Also available in the Guys Read Library of Great Reading

GUYS READ

TERRIFYING TALES

EDITED AND WITH AN INTRODUCTION BY
JON SCIESZKA

STORIES BY

KELLY BARNHILL, MICHAEL BUCKLEY, ADAM GIDWITZ, ADELE GRIFFIN AND LISA BROWN, CLAIRE LEGRAND, NIKKI LOFTIN, DANIEL JOSÉ OLDER, DAV PILKEY, R.L. STINE, AND RITA WILLIAMS-GARCIA

WITH ILLUSTRATIONS BY
GRIS GRIMLY

WALDEN POND PRESS
An Imprint of HarperCollinsPublishers

Walden Pond Press is an imprint of HarperCollins Publishers.
Walden Pond Press and the skipping stone logo are trademarks and registered
trademarks of Walden Media, LLC.

Library of Congress Control Number: 2015938892
ISBN 978-0-06-238558-1 (trade bdg.) — ISBN 978-0-06-238557-4 (pbk.)

Typography by Joel Tippie
15 16 17 18 19   PC/RRDH   10 9 8 7 6 5 4 3 2 1
❖
First Edition

CONTENTS

GUYS READ

TERRIFYING
TALES

BEFORE WE BEGIN . . .

Come on in.

Closer.

Don't be afraid.

It's just a bunch of stories.

What could be so terrifying about that?

Well—maybe your sister's footless ghost appearing in the middle of the night. Maybe an imaginary friend . . . who might not be so imaginary. Or maybe tattoos that suddenly and very painfully start etching themselves all over your body!

Sorry.

I got a little carried away.

Heart pounding a little faster. Breathing a bit ragged.

You think you can take more?

What if your little brother vanished? What if water spirits came out of the river and haunted your every moment? What if your local librarian turned out to be something more (and something more disgustingly creepy) than a librarian? What if you actually had to tell the brother you always wished for, "Don't eat the baby"?

Palms sweating a bit now.

And I haven't even told you where, and in what shape, a young girl finds her missing sisters.

Yikes!

It's just a fairy tale, just a fairy tale, just a fairy tale, I keep telling myself.

The writers in this volume of your Guys Read Library of Great Reading may have done too good a job. We told them to go all out to shake you up, freak you out, and just completely terrify you.

Did they ever.

I'm not sure why some people like to read scary stories. Many experts say it might be a way of conquering fears in practice. Other experts say they love the rush of excitement, and the relief when the terror is over.

I say these people are nuts.

And if you really want to be stuck sleeping with the light

on for the next week or two, take a good long look at that Gris Grimly cover.

Whoa.

Oh, and one more bit you might learn from this volume: You know that crazy old lady down the block? The one you suspect might actually not be crazy, but horrifically evil?

You're right.

Neck hairs now straight up.

Good luck, and please enjoy these terrifying tales at your own risk.

Jon Scieszka

MR. SHOCKY
BY MICHAEL BUCKLEY

I hear my little brother's terrified screams a block away. I pump my pedals as hard as I can and steer my bike toward home. Tearing through my yard, I destroy my mother's azalea bush on my way to the back of the house. There I find him clinging to the highest rung of a rotting rope ladder. It leads to my long-abandoned tree house, a place he should know better than to explore. It's been threatening to collapse for months, and worse, it's dizzyingly high above the ground. If he falls . . .

"Hold on, Dylan!" I shout, ditching the bike and sprinting to the base of the tree, praying he won't plummet to the ground before I can get to him. He's only four years old. How did he even get up there?

"Tyler, I'm slipping," he sobs when he hears my voice.

"I'm coming up!" I say, trying to sound as confident as possible. I scamper up the remains of the rope ladder as quickly as I can, hearing its strained fibers groaning against my weight. I nearly fall when one of the rungs splits, but I manage to hold on and regain my balance. A moment later I have Dylan safely in my arms and we climb back down.

"You know you're not allowed in the tree house," I cry once we are on firm ground. It comes out loud and angry, and he breaks into fresh tears. I hug him and tell him I'm not mad. To be honest, though, I'm fuming—but not at him. Ella, his babysitter for all of a week, is supposed to be watching him. I lead him into the house and the two of us find her lying on the couch, texting furiously on her phone. She's oblivious to what just happened, and completely surprised. I know I'm only twelve, but I fire her right then and there. I doubt Mom and Dad will disagree with me when they get home. She may be a grade older than me, but she's clearly in over her head. Ella is a complete idiot.

After she turns over her keys and the door slams in her face, I take Dylan upstairs to the bathroom and put him in the tub. A bubble bath always calms him down, especially if I use the lavender baby soap he loves. Mom swears by it. Soon he's covered in suds and playing with his tub toys, his brush with death a distant memory.

"Dylan, why did you go up to the tree house? You know that's off-limits."

"I was playing and he said it would be okay. He said the tree house was full of toys and candy."

"Who said that?" I ask, wondering if some neighbor kid lured him into this dumb stunt.

"Mr. Shocky told me to do it," he says. "He's my friend."

Dylan is in bed and my parents are taking turns chewing out the ex-babysitter on the phone. When they're done, we sit down at the table to make a plan. Both of them work full-time jobs, so until they can hire a replacement, I'm going into the babysitting business, which means picking Dylan up from preschool right after school. It also means no Minecraft at Jake's, or skateboarding at the park, or working on my free throws. But he's my brother. And I actually like hanging out with him, mostly. Besides, Jake's house always smells like vegetable soup.

"Mom, did you tell Dylan about Mr. Shocky?" I ask as I watch her load the dishwasher.

She flinches, as if stung by a bee, then stares at me with a mixture of concern and fear. "No. You know how I feel about that. Why?"

My father pokes his head into the kitchen. "Tyler? Should we be worried?"

Mr. Shocky is a sore subject in my house. He was my imaginary friend when I was Dylan's age, and he stuck around a bit longer . . . well, actually a lot longer than is probably normal for kids. I was a loner when I was little, and pretty shy, and so I invented a playmate. Mr. Shocky was with me until I was almost nine, and at that point my parents took me to see Dr. Rosen, a child psychiatrist who prescribed pills and taught me how to make real friends. It wasn't easy but it worked. It has been three years, and I feel good. I don't have to take the meds anymore, and I haven't seen Mr. Shocky in a long time.

"I'm fine," I say, trying to diffuse the tension in the room. This conversation feels like an overstretched rubber band that is about to snap and fling us all into space. "Dylan told me that Mr. Shocky got him to climb the ladder. I've never said anything about him, so I thought maybe he overheard you two talking."

My "break with reality" is a frequent topic of conversation in their room late at night when they think I can't hear them. I hate that three years later it's still coming up. They treat me like I'm fragile, like an expensive vase resting on a wobbly table. They don't need to be worried. Mr. Shocky is behind me.

My father flashes my mother a knowing look. "I'm

tearing that tree house down this weekend."

My mother nods. "It's about time."

The next day I pick Dylan up at his preschool. He is covered in finger paints and a huge smile. They must let the kids go crazy with the art supplies. The rest of him is smeared with glitter and purple glue stick. Making art projects is Dylan's favorite thing to do, so I'm happy for him, but man, what a mess.

He's beaming with pride today, holding a painting out to me with his sticky red and purple hands. It's his latest masterpiece.

"Wow!" I say when I look at his treasure. Standing on a hill covered in yellow flowers is Dylan, all smiles and a mop of red hair. Next to him is a man, or rather the silhouette of a man, a tall black figure sporting two fiery red eyes and a long pointy tail. "It's awesome, buddy, but who is this person standing next to you?"

"Mr. Shocky."

My head starts to pound and my heart is rising up into my throat. "Dylan, where did you hear about Mr. Shocky?"

"Nowhere," he says. "I told you, he's my friend. He plays with me every day. He says he wants to be with me, always."

I shudder and break into a sweat. The echo of my younger

self is bouncing around in my ears. I said the same exact thing to Dr. Rosen when I was his patient. I can still see his sad, sympathetic smile, the funny green pills he gave me that made me sleepy, his endless insistence that Mr. Shocky was not real. A panic rolls through me as I imagine Dylan taking my place in those therapy sessions. I see him swallowing those little green pills. I can't let him go through that. I have to protect him, even if it's from himself.

"Mr. Shocky is not real," I snap, wadding his painting into a ball.

Dylan bursts into tears.

"Now I know why he's mad at you," my brother cries. "He said you're mean and a bad friend. And he's right."

I heat up some leftover spaghetti and feed Dylan, then get him into the tub again to scrub off the layers of finger paint. He won't talk to me. He's still angry about the painting, so we sit silently and watch an episode of *Wild Kratts* on TV. Afterward we lie in my parents' bed and I read him books about a pig and an elephant who are buddies until he falls asleep. I carry him into his own room and tuck him in.

There are paintings all over the walls. He's proudly taped them up, his own personal art gallery. In every painting there's a long black figure with red eyes and a tail.

Mr. Shocky is creeping around again—poking into my life, challenging the walls Dr. Rosen and I built around my sanity. But this time it's different. Dylan's version of our mutual friend isn't how I remember Mr. Shocky, or at least not how my brain conjured him back then. It gives me hope that I'm not losing it again, that this is just an odd coincidence between two brothers. But I need to be sure.

When Mom and Dad get home, they check on Dylan while I grab a flashlight from the junk drawer and creep into the backyard. I pad across the cool grass to the old oak tree and shine a beam on my tree house. It's been there for years, long before my parents bought the house, but decay is having its way with it. Rusty nails are popping out and wooden planks are rotting. My mother declared it off-limits after she climbed up into it looking for the neighbors' cat. A floorboard cracked under her weight and that was it—no more tree house. I wasn't even allowed to go up and get the stuff I kept there, little boy treasures that meant the world to me.

I carefully climb the rope ladder and scamper inside. I can no longer stand all the way up, having grown since my last visit, so I crawl on hands and knees searching with the flashlight and trying to avoid anything sharp. My stuff is still here, though strewn around in a mess by several harsh winters and rainy springs. A small stack of waterlogged Donald Duck comics that has toppled over; an old sock filled with marbles; my father's favorite flip-flops, the ones he frequently tears the house apart looking for. There is a box filled with action figures and a wooden sword used for fighting off pirate invasions. At the bottom is my own art collection. Like Dylan, I loved to draw, and kept every art project I made. I sort through the brittle paper until I find the one I want; a portrait almost identical to the one Dylan gave me earlier that day. It's me, standing in a field of golden flowers, and next to me is a tall man. He has a huge grin on his face and the two of us are holding hands, but, unlike Dylan's haunting black figure, this one is made of rainbow colors. This was my "Mr. Shocky." No darkness, no threatening eyes. Dylan's friend is something else entirely. I'm not going crazy. My imaginary friend has not returned. The walls are strong and tall.

Dylan wakes me up in the dimmest hours of the night. I can barely see him through fuzzy eyes, only his outline against the yellow hallway light.

"You made Mr. Shocky sad," Dylan says.

"Dylan, why are you out of bed?"

"You stopped playing with him. You hurt his feelings. He says he's going to hurt me if you won't be his friend again." Dylan's voice sounds odd, high-pitched, almost cartoony but angry. "You just left him. You didn't even say good-bye."

I take him by the hand and lead him back to his room. "You're having a bad dream," I say, then wait for him to go back to sleep. When he is safe and sound, I creep back into the hallway and into the bathroom. I flip on the light and splash my face with some water. I hate the idea of Dylan having to suffer through Dr. Rosen's treatment, but I can't keep what I know from Mom and Dad. He needs help. I will tell them in the morning. Let the kid have one more night of feeling normal.

The next day I wake to find Dr. Rosen in our living room. He sits still and tall in a high-backed chair with his hands in his lap and a concerned expression on his face. My parents sit on the very edge of the couch, nervous and jumpy.

"Hello, Tyler. It's good to see you again," the doctor says in his most calming voice. I know it well. He used it during most of our conversations, especially in the beginning.

"Nice to see you, too," I say, but my eyes are going back and forth from Mom to Dad.

He nods. "Your parents tell me there's been some trouble," he says.

"Yes, I've noticed it for a few days, but it's under control and—"

"Tyler, what did we agree to long ago? We promised to be honest with each other. I'm your friend and I have had a lot of success making you feel better, so there's no need to hide anything or feel embarrassed. Why not just tell me what is happening? The sooner you open up, the better you're going to feel." Dr. Rosen's hands come together in front of his chin, making a steeple that holds up his face.

"Wait! This isn't about me," I say, suddenly confused.

"You're not seeing Mr. Shocky anymore?"

"No!"

"You're not acting out parts of your daydreams again?" my mother cries, then breaks into tears.

"Mom?"

"Tyler, are you really going to stand there and act like you didn't do it?" my father barks.

"Do what?"

Dr. Rosen waves his hand to quiet the conversation.

"Tyler, let's go take a look at your brother's room," he says.

"Why?" I ask. "Where is Dylan? Did something happen?"

"Dylan is safe," the doctor says as he stands and leads us all upstairs. My father opens my brother's bedroom door and I step inside only to see a disaster. Everything is trashed. Dylan's stuffed animals are torn to shreds. His bed is tipped over and a long, jagged slash in the mattress spills stuffing all over the floor. His curtains are ripped off the walls and now lie in clumps on the floor. Every toy he has is smashed into thousands of tiny plastic pieces. Scrawled on the wall in big black letters are the words "YOU ABANDONED ME."

My head is spinning so fast I worry it might pop off my shoulders. "What were you thinking when you did this?" my father demands.

"Dad, I didn't—"

"Don't lie to me!" he shouts. He has never yelled at me like this and it startles me.

"Let's stay calm," Dr. Rosen says, coming to my defense. "When Tyler says he didn't do this, he isn't lying. He truly believes he is innocent. His brain won't let him remember. He's suffering from what is called a dissociative state."

"A what?" my mother asks.

"His mind won't let him deal with his illness, so it erases

his actions from his memory. It's a way of protecting himself from having to deal with what he's feeling. In other words, Tyler, clearly angry about the loss of his imaginary friend, is acting out on Mr. Shocky's behalf."

"That's not what I'm doing!" I cry. I can't believe they are blaming me for all this mess, and now they're saying I'm doing it without even knowing.

"I'll need more time with your son to know for sure," Dr. Rosen says, "but that's my best educated guess."

"Can you fix him?" my father asks.

The psychiatrist cringes, as if the answer gives him great pain. "He's not a broken chair. But if he's willing to do the work, my center is his best chance at recovery."

"Center?" my mother blubbers.

"A home for troubled children," the doctor explains as he looks right at me.

"I don't want to go," I beg, backing away from them.

"Right now you're too dangerous to be around Dylan," my mother says.

"I would never hurt him," I plead with my family. They have to believe me.

"You lured him into the tree house, Tyler," my father snaps. "Ella told us."

"I did not! She wasn't paying attention—"

"Ella says she never let Dylan out of her sight until you came home," my mother says.

"Would Tyler live at this center?" my father asks the doctor.

"He'd have to," Dr. Rosen says. "It's probably his only chance at a normal life."

I panic and dart through my bedroom door, slamming it behind me and locking it tight. Why did I come in here? Now I'm trapped. I pace the room while they pound on the door and demand I open it.

"I won't go with him!" I shout through the door.

Suddenly, I catch some movement in the mirror on my bedroom wall. At first I think it's a shadow, some trick of the light, but then I realize it's stalking toward me. I can hear the skittering of its toenails on the hardwood floor. And then, in the mirror, I can see it towering over me from behind. It's disgustingly thin, at least twice my height, and black as death, but it's not a person. It's a hole, a sucking wound in the body of reality, and the nearer it gets to me, the more I feel the pull of that hole. It grasps at my T-shirt, determined to pull me into it, drag me down, drown me. And its tail, long and ebony, ends in a vicious point, but when it touches me, it's so cold it burns. It wraps around my throat, squeezing like a snake, stealing my breath. But it's his eyes that cause my body to tremble. They are red like angry blisters, full of rage and insanity, and looking right at me.

"What do you want?" I stammer.

"You threw me away, Tyler." Its voice is like dead leaves rustling in an abandoned graveyard. "I want revenge."

Somehow I muster the strength to turn and face it before its tail can choke the life out of me.

"I did not throw you away!"

But Mr. Shocky is not there. I am alone. Is Dr. Rosen right? Am I losing it? Am I doing terrible things, then forcing myself to forget them? Did I destroy my baby brother's room? Did I lure him into the tree house? I can't be sure anymore, and I don't have the luxury of not knowing, not with Dylan in the room next to mine. I unlock my bedroom door and swing it open.

"I'll go with you," I say. "Just make me better."

New Beginnings Center isn't so bad. In fact, aside from all the meditation and daily group therapy sessions, it is a lot like sleepaway camp. The grounds are big. There is a soccer field, a basketball court, and a pool. The library has some decent books, and I sort of enjoy the fact that I get to wear pajamas every day.

The other kids in the facility are there for various reasons;

some have panic attacks, others are just sad. Then there are the other kids, the dangerous ones, like the boy who likes to start fires, and a girl whose night terrors keep her up. They stay in a different wing than me. One night I saw a kid run down the hall that connects that wing to mine while a beefy security guard chased her. She screamed when she was caught. The next day the guard's face was covered in scratches and bandages. Other than that, though, things have been pretty calm.

My parents visit twice a week, and we go on long walks to the greenhouse and to the pond.

"How's Dylan?" I always ask.

Their smiles are tight when they tell me he is fine. They still think I'm a danger to him, but they never admit it. One time they gave me a few of his little drawings, made just for me. I treasure every one, keeping them in my bedside table drawer. I take them out whenever I'm feeling lonely or frustrated, which is most of the time.

"How are we feeling today?" Dr. Rosen asks me during group therapy. This session is called "the talking dog" because we pass a stuffed dog toy from one person to the next. Whoever has the dog can talk. If you don't, you have to keep quiet and listen. Today, I find the dog in my lap.

"I feel good," I say. To be honest, I don't feel much different than I did the day they locked me up in here, but I am learning to play the game, and staying positive is part of it. If I have any hope of ever getting out, I need to keep a smile on my face.

"It's been thirty days since you joined us," Dr. Rosen says. "Have you had any visits from Mr. Shocky?"

I shake my head. I haven't seen a hint of either the rainbow or monster version of my imaginary friend. "Not a peep."

"How does that feel, Tyler?"

Before I can answer, the door opens and a pale-faced girl charges into the room. Her hair is ratty and streaked with platinum white strands. Her eyes have dark circles under them, making it look like she crawled out of somewhere dark. She plops down into an empty seat and tucks her feet under herself, curling in tight as if the rest of us are contagious.

Dr. Rosen's face darkens and he shifts in his chair, but he doesn't scold her for being late. Last week he gave me a lecture because I showed up a minute past the hour. This girl is strolling in five minutes before we head to lunch.

"Tyler, could you continue discussing your current successes?" Dr. Rosen says to me.

"Current successes?" The girl laughs. "How successful could he be if he's stuck in this loony bin? Right, Doc?"

Dr. Rosen frowns and the girl laughs at him. Rosen looks down into his notes, refusing to take her bait. I'm stunned. Who is this girl, and why is Rosen letting her disrupt the session?

She turns her attention back to me.

"So, you're crazy, huh?"

I have no idea how to answer that question, so I just shake my head.

"C'mon, kid! Why are you here?" she cries.

"When I was little, I had an imaginary friend that I couldn't let go of, but I know he isn't real and I made him go away."

"That's encouraging news," Dr. Rosen says.

The girl shoots the doctor a vicious look. "Imaginary, huh? Is that what you told him?"

Dr. Rosen shifts uncomfortably again, but he remains quiet.

She leans back in her seat and chuckles. "Is it that you couldn't let go of him—or that he *wouldn't* let go of you?"

I toss and turn in my bed, unable to get the angry girl out of my head. What did she mean when she said Mr. Shocky wouldn't let me go? My mind tells me to forget about her, that she's just some sick kid who enjoys freaking out the other patients. I know the type. The center has dozens of jerks like her, yet something about her can't be forgotten. Maybe it was the way she sneered at Dr. Rosen, or maybe it was the "I know something you don't know" look in her eyes. I'm so wound up I almost don't hear the soft scraping noise near the door to my room. In the moonlight I watch a slip of paper slide under the crack. I get up and snatch it off the floor. It's a note scribbled in crayon.

If you want the truth come to the art room.—Esmeralda

Esmeralda. I have no proof that it's from the girl in group therapy, but something tells me it is. When I open the door and peer out, there's no one there. I look down the hall. Around the far corner is the art room, in the same wing as the really troubled and dangerous kids. I'm sure that's where they keep her. I should ignore her, but my curiosity is on fire. There's no way I'm going to get any sleep until I find out what she wants. I decide to follow her.

It isn't easy. I dart from door to door to avoid the orderlies and nurses, and hide in the bathroom from the snooping security guard. When I finally get to the art room door, I'm a nervous wreck. I hurry in and find myself in blackness. A tiny sliver of moonbeam reveals three figures waiting for me.

"How did you guys get in here without being seen?" I

say as I struggle to catch my breath.

"I told you he'd come," a voice says. I recognize it as the girl.

"This is a waste of time, Esmeralda," the smallest of the figures says. "He won't believe us and besides, it's his problem, not ours."

"Stop whining, Chad," the biggest shadow complains. "We all agreed to help him."

"What's going on here?" I demand.

There is a click and a small table lamp illuminates everything. For the first time I can see the group. Esmeralda looks as tired and washed-out as before. Her friend Chad is a sour little guy with a big nose and thick glasses. Their friend is big and puffy with a face like a baby.

"Depends. You said you have an imaginary friend problem," Esmeralda says.

"Oh, this is a joke," I say.

"It's not a joke," the big kid says. "What is yours called?"

"I'm out of here," I fume. I'm not going to stand here and let them laugh at me. But in a flash Esmeralda blocks my way.

"Just hear us out," she begs.

"Awww, let him go," Chad says as he pushes his glasses up his nose. "He doesn't want our help."

"He just needs proof. Show him, Nicholas," Esmeralda says to the big kid.

Nicholas leads me to a mirror on the wall. When we are in front of it, he looks to me and says, "Don't freak out." Then he turns to the mirror. "Hey, Davenport, it's me, Nicholas."

"I really don't—"

"Be quiet or the gjenganger won't come," Chad snaps.

"What's a gjenganger?"

"It's what you call an imaginary friend," Nicholas explains, then turns back to the mirror. "Come on, Davenport. Come on out."

There's a nervous shift in the air and I'm suddenly not so sure this is a joke. I hear a thumping sound that sends tremors into my feet. My throat goes dry and tightens into a knot. There's another thump and I see a pencil bounce on a nearby desk. My brain says this is my imagination, but my senses are telling me it's more than that. Still, they can't prepare me for Davenport's arrival. Suddenly, he's there, right behind me in the reflection, a massive, towering beast of muscle, matted hair, and bloody claws. I can't see its face, but its breath is a furnace on the back of my neck that grows hotter and closer with every passing moment. I'm losing the battle against the scream that's rising up through my body.

"Don't panic, just be cool," Nicholas says as he turns his gaze back to the monster's reflection. "Davenport, this is my new friend, Tyler," he says in a cheerful voice.

Davenport's roar blasts me with rage and hostility. My instinct is to run, but Nicholas grabs me by the arm and holds me tight.

"No, he's not going to replace you, Davenport. You're still my favorite. I just want you to meet him. Tyler can play games with us, but only when you say it's okay."

The creature grunts as if he is debating whether to rip my head off my shoulders or not. I get the impression he doesn't want to share Nicholas with anyone.

"Only when you say it's okay," Nicholas repeats to the beast, then nudges me, letting me know it is okay to move away from the mirror.

"What is that thing?" I whimper, once I can no longer see it.

"We told you," Chad cries. "It's called a gjenganger, a creature that has found a way out of imagination and into our world."

"How?"

"Who knows? But once they're free, oh man! They latch onto a kid like a parasite and they don't let go."

"They're looking for affection. They feed on it and

normally they're harmless," Esmeralda says. "Usually when the child gets to a certain age, the gjenganger crawls back to where it came from and waits for the next kid to come along, but sometimes—"

"What?" I beg.

"Sometimes they don't want to go back," she says. "That's what happened with yours."

"What do you call it, anyway?" Nicholas asks.

"Mr. Shocky," I whisper.

"It's probably too late to get rid of him now," Chad says. "He's got his hooks in you."

"No, I got rid of him before. Dr. Rosen helped, but somehow he came back and he's with my brother."

"And he's angry?" Esmeralda says.

I nod. "How do you know so much about these things?"

Esmeralda turns to the others. "We have to help him before it's too late. Who's with me?"

Suddenly, there's a bang and the overhead lights come on. I spin toward the door, sure that Davenport or something even worse has come for us.

"You three should be in bed," Dr. Rosen says. He's smiling at us like we're a bunch of incorrigible pranksters.

"I told him the truth," Esmeralda says. "I told him about the gjenganger."

Dr. Rosen's face puckers up like he has bitten into a lemon. It's the first time I have ever seen him angry. "I wish you hadn't done that."

"It's not right that you lie to him," Esmeralda continues.

"Esmeralda, you know as well as I do that if I was honest with Tyler, then he would never free himself from that thing. The only way to send it back is to reject its very existence. Now that Tyler knows Mr. Shocky is real, he'll—"

The world slides sideways. "Wait! Mr. Shocky is real? You made me think I was crazy!"

"I had to," the doctor cries. "And it works! Mr. Shocky was gone for three years. This is the first time a gjenganger has come back."

"That thing is with my brother," I cry. "I have to get home."

"I won't let you go," Dr. Rosen says. "There are other ways to get rid of these creatures and—"

"You can't stop me."

"Yes, I can," he snaps, his face as red as blood. He reaches into his pocket and takes out a whistle then blasts a screaming note into the air. "Security will be here in just a moment to get you back into bed. We're going to have to adjust your medications."

Esmeralda steps up to the doctor. "This has gone on

long enough, Tommy. Nicholas, get us out of here."

"Davenport, make a door!" Nicholas cries.

I hear a huff, then the sound of claws rapidly clicking on the marble floor. A second later there is a huge crash, a cloud of dust, and a massive hole in the wall in front of us. I stand still, dumbfounded and unable to act. My brain just can't accept what I am witnessing and yet, it's real. For the first time in my life I know that I am perfectly healthy.

And then we run.

The four of us (well, five, if you count Davenport) race into the night, charging through the chilly air with little direction and even less light. We tumble into the forest that surrounds the center and stamp around for a while until we come across a road. About a half a mile on we discover a train station and make a mad dash for the platform, where a train is preparing to leave. Luckily, one of its stops is my hometown. We find seats in the back of the car to avoid the ticket collector and move frequently so as not to let on that we don't have tickets.

The sun is coming up when we arrive. Once outside, we jog toward my house, a good half mile away. Each step is a mounting anxiety. Am I too late? Has Mr. Shocky already hurt Dylan? And then the biggest question of all.

"How do we stop him?"

"There's a way," Esmeralda says. "Gjengangere are creatures of imagination, so you fight it with imagination."

"I'm confused."

Chad rolls his eyes. "If you're going to destroy Mr. Shocky, you have to build a weapon in your mind that can kill him. We'll show you how to drag it out into the real world, but make it a good one. You'll only get one chance. If you fail . . ."

"What? What happens?"

"They fight back. Mine . . ." Chad looks like he might cry. It's the first expression on his face I have seen that isn't disgust or impatience. He tries to continue but then breaks into tears and runs ahead of us.

"Chad's imaginary friend was called Zaxx. He wouldn't go away and when Chad fought back, it attacked his mother and father," Nicholas explains.

"Attacked?"

"It killed them."

I gasp and my stomach turns sour. I'm sure I'm going to vomit.

"It's why I have learned to live with Davenport," Nicholas says. "I could never figure out how to create these imaginary weapons and it's not worth the risk anyway. As long as

I give it enough attention, I don't have to worry."

"We're wasting time," Esmeralda cries. "You need to be thinking of your weapon. Mr. Shocky knows we're coming and he'll be ready."

When we race into my house, my parents are in a panic and Dr. Rosen is waiting.

"We won't let you stop us," I say to him.

Dr. Rosen shakes his head. "I'm not here to stop you. I came to help. I told your parents the truth and . . . they're not yet ready to accept this story."

"What is going on?" my father shouts. "Has the whole world lost its mind?"

"Where's Dylan?" I beg.

"In his room. He's still sleeping," my mother says, and before she can stop us, we all race upstairs. I push the door open and on the other side is my baby brother, dangling in midair, held off the ground by an invisible force. He is in hysterics, sobbing and terrified, kicking his little legs in a vain attempt to touch the floor.

"Tyler!" he wails.

"Don't worry, I'm not going to let Mr. Shocky hurt you, little man," I say, though I still have no clue how I'm going to stop him.

Dr. Rosen seems to understand my fears. "You can't see him, can you? That's my fault, Tyler. He's there, but you have to forget everything I told you if you want to see him. You have to throw away all the skills I helped you learn, knock down the walls we built. I thought they would protect you, but I was wrong. Mr. Shocky is real and until you accept that fact, you won't be able to hurt him."

"How do I stop something my brain won't let me see?"

Esmeralda takes my hand. "You can see me."

I stare into her dark eyes and suddenly understand. "You're one of them?"

She nods, then tilts her head toward Dr. Rosen. "I'm with him, have been since he was three."

"Why are you helping me?"

"That thing should have moved on. Those are the rules. He's breaking them," Esmeralda says.

"But you stuck around," I say, gesturing to the doctor.

"He asked me to. It's different," she says. "Now, you have to accept that Mr. Shocky is real. It's your only chance."

And then, before my eyes, I see Mr. Shocky—not my rainbow friend, but the angry, black, and broken creature he has become. I see his bloodred eyes and his wicked tail whipping around the room. I see his black talons wrapped around my brother's neck, and I close my eyes and concentrate, searching my imagination for a weapon that will kill him where he stands.

Twenty years later . . .

I wish I could say it worked, but it didn't. The nagging voices in my head, the ones that sounded just like my parents and friends and Dr. Rosen, the ones that told me that it was all in my head, were just too loud. When my weapon failed to appear, Chad attacked Mr. Shocky but got tossed across the room. Dr. Rosen tried and failed, too. Nicholas sent in Davenport, and even Esmeralda fought. But none of us were a match for my blackest nightmare.

So, like Nicholas, I was forced to make a deal. To keep the people I love safe, I promised to be Mr. Shocky's friend forever. And in exchange, he promised not to hurt my family.

Now I play hide-and-seek with him every day. Mr. Shocky and I put on little plays and draw pictures and crawl around on monkey bars, and as long as I keep doing what he wants, then he's happy. Unfortunately, I lost all my real friends. I can't keep a job, or a relationship. Everyone thinks I've lost my mind, a thirty-two-year-old man who spends half his day talking to someone who isn't there. But that's probably for the best. People should keep their distance from me. I don't want anyone getting hurt.

Chad checks in from time to time, though I haven't heard from Nicholas in a while. Last time we spoke, he said he was finally going to tell Davenport to go away. I went by his house once, but there was no one there.

Dr. Rosen calls every couple days, but he's getting on in years. He's worried about me. He says that he's had patients who were hurt when their imaginary friends got bored with them, when they got too old to climb trees and run races and pretend to be pirates in rickety tree houses. He worries that someday Mr. Shocky will hurt me when I'm too old for his games.

Esmeralda is helping me prepare. She comes to me sometimes, still the washed-out twelve-year-old girl I met at the clinic. She's been teaching me to embrace my imagination. It's slowly starting to work. Last night I dragged a penny out of a daydream and into the real world. It's small but it's a start, and who knows? With more practice I might be able to make a sword, or even my own Davenport to rip Mr. Shocky limb from limb.

But, for now, I have to get to the park. My imaginary friend wants me to push him on the swings.

LICORICE NEEDLES
BY NIKKI LOFTIN

My mouth is full of tarry black candy. Licorice needles, Mrs. Carlson calls them. She gave me a few long pieces, said I could have the whole jar if I didn't mess up reading today. It's strange-tasting stuff, and it separates into lots of little strands as I chew, sticking in between my teeth. She's fallen asleep at the kitchen table, and I wonder if there's anywhere I can spit it out. But it's my first time at her house, and I want to make a good impression on the old lady. Mom's decided I'm going to go read to her every day after school until I start passing seventh grade English, or until Mrs. Carlson tells her I've improved enough. If she likes me, maybe she'll let me go early today.

"You forgot to say thank you." Her voice makes me jump.

There goes the good impression. "Sorry. I thought you fell asleep." It's hard to tell. She wears these big dark glasses because of her weak eyes. "She's mostly blind," my mom said this morning. "And she agreed to tutor you for free. It's a win-win! Your reading will get better, and she'll be able to enjoy her books again." Then she raced off to work.

"Start reading." Mrs. Carlson lays a cold hand on my wrist. Her skin is crinkly and weird, with blue veins roping all across the tops of her fingers. Fragile looking. If anyone shook her hand too hard, I think, the veins might pop and she could bleed to death. Old people are gross. I open the book she set down in front of me.

"It was many and many a year ago,
In a kingdom by the sea,
That a maiden there lived whom you may know
By the name of Annabel Lee."

It's by this guy Edgar Allen Poe. It's long and boring, but at least there aren't any hard words. I pause anyway. There's a girl who lives down the street with the same name, Annabel Lee. She's about three years younger than me, and I saw her over at Mrs. Carlson's the day before, picking some big flowers out of the yard. It left a sort of bare patch in the front garden. I wonder if the old lady saw her, too.

"Don't stop," Mrs. Carlson whispers hoarsely. "Third stanza, first four lines."

"And this was the reason that, long ago,
In this kingdom by the sea,
A wind blew out of a cloud, chilling
My beautiful Annabel Lee."

"Stealing my flowers," Mrs. Carlson mutters as I finish. "Hmph." She smiles, then pulls the book out of my hands and slips me a different paper. "Now, quickly, this one," she says. "The whole thing. Exactly as it's written."

This one's harder. It's in old-fashioned cursive writing, with lots of curlicues. *Her* handwriting? I'm not sure. The words are hard—I don't even know what most of them mean—and I stumble a bit, but not too bad.

"Purloin, pillage, pilfer, plunder,
hand that takes must suffer thunder
feel the pinch of consequence
thieving part be severed hence."

Before I even get the last word out, she shoves a scrap of newspaper toward me. "Read the weather report, quickly, quickly!"

I shake my head, wondering how Mom could have thought this lady was going to help me get better at reading. I'm pretty certain she thought I'd be reading real books. "Quickly, now!" She sounds really upset I've stopped, so I read as fast as I can. "Tomorrow's high, fifty-two degrees. Thunderstorms expected by late afternoon, with possible hail and high winds."

I don't see any date on the paper, but I know it's not today's. It never gets that cold in September. Should I tell her? I decide not to. I guess old ladies collect old newspapers. Sad.

"Are we done?" I ask Mrs. Carlson, but she doesn't hear me. She's doing something with the papers I read, moving her hands over them like she's feeling for Braille bumps or something. Her hands are all shaky.

It must stink, being old. I'm going to start skydiving when I'm sixty, or base jumping off volcanoes. Something dangerous and cool that probably also means I won't live to see nursing home age. "You did very well, Jeremiah. Time for a treat," Mrs. Carlson says, and crosses the kitchen to cut me a piece of homemade spice cake. I eat it fast to get the licorice taste out of my mouth. It's way better than those needles. At least the old lady can bake.

The next day, Mrs. Carlson has me reading from a book, a hard one about Russian legends, when I hear a giant thunderclap. It actually shakes the table, the whole house. "Whoa!" I yell. Car alarms are ringing down the street. "Just a sec, Mrs. C." I run for the door.

It's so strange. The sky on one side of the neighborhood is blue and clear, but behind Mrs. Carlson's house, and stretching back into the neighborhood, it's all black clouds and . . .

"Hail?" The cold wind whips past me, and I watch for a few minutes as trees bend crazily all around. Is it a tornado? "Where did this come from?"

I feel Mrs. Carlson's hand on my shoulder. "Listen," she whispers. I hear it, too. Over the sounds of the car alarms, there's something else . . . a siren. An ambulance.

"Good," Mrs. Carlson murmurs.

Good? I wonder if I should tell Mom how nutso this old lady is, as I help her back into the house. But then I smell the pumpkin pie she has waiting for the end of the lesson, and I know I'm not going to tell Mom anything. Reading stupid stuff to a crazy lady who bakes all the time? It could be worse.

* * *

Wednesday at lunchtime all anyone can talk about is the storm. "My dad said the wind knocked the power pole down three streets over from your house, Jeremiah," my friend Pedro says.

"Yeah, and when it did," Max interrupts, "it made the power go on and off, and this girl who lives at the end of my cul-de-sac had just dropped a spoon down the garbage disposal, and she reached in to get it, and then the power came back on with her hand in it and—clakglukclakgluk-clakgluk! he yells, swinging his arm back and forth like it's being torn apart, and spraying us all with tiny flecks of cheeseburger as he shouts.

After that, Pedro and I take turns knuckle thumping him on the head for being gross, and it isn't until the end of lunch that I think to ask who the girl was.

"You know her," Max says. "Annabel Lee Lindstrom."

"Annabel Lee?" I know it's a coincidence—me reading that poem, then the stuff about severed hands to Mrs. Carlson, and now this—but I feel sick all of a sudden, like I've been caught cheating on a test. "It can't be."

"What?" Max says, shaking me out of my crazy thoughts. "Did you like her or something?" He laughs. "Too bad you'll never be able to hold her hand now."

"You idiot!" I chase him around the table, trying to thump his head again, until the bell rings.

Annabel will be all right, I tell myself on my way to class. Maybe it wasn't that bad. Max said she lost all her fingers, her whole hand practically, but he likes to exaggerate.

That afternoon, on my way to Mrs. Carlson's, I pass a couple of guys I know. They're walking around with giant bags of pick-a-mix candies, laughing, having fun like I used to after school. They keep tossing their candy wrappers on the ground, and it makes me mad . . . mainly because it reminds me of how trashed my life is.

I've got to get out of these dumb lessons.

For the next hour and a half, Mrs. Carlson has me read the first chapters of a book called *Great Expectations*. It's possibly the most boring book I've ever tried to read. By the time I struggle to the end of the second chapter, even Mrs. Carlson looks like she wants to throw the book across the room. I wonder if I can figure some way to leave early. Maybe I can fake being sick?

But something about Mrs. Carlson tells me lying to her wouldn't be a good idea. Probably some leftover meanness from being an English teacher for fifty years.

At dinner, I ask Mom when I can stop the lessons.

"When you're making a B in English, Jeremiah Denton," she says, and shakes her head. "I'm just glad Mrs. Carlson moved in three months ago. If she hadn't agreed to do this . . . well, let's just say your birthday present money would all be going to the House of Tutors."

She looks tired but tries to smile, so I suck it up and don't say anything else about Mrs. Carlson's shaky hands, her crazy lessons . . . or what happened to Annabel Lee.

The next day, I'm on the bus to Mrs. Carlson's, all set to try to talk her out of *Great Expectations*. But I completely forget about that when we pull up, and she's in her front yard, on her hand and knees, feeling around for . . . candy wrappers? Yes. There are candy wrappers and plastic grocery bags all over her yard. The wind is blowing, and I wonder if the wrappers are the same ones the guys I saw were tossing around.

"Mrs. C? Are you okay?" I ask.

"No," she says. "Some delinquent children decided to suffocate my grass with their plastic filth." Grabbing onto my arm, she gets to her feet slowly, the plastic bags dangling from her free hand. Suffocating her grass? It's a weird way to think of it, but when I take the bags to throw in her trash can, I see one of them—a pick-a-mix candy one, sure enough—has that warning printed on it about keeping kids from sticking plastic bags over their heads or whatever. I always wondered what kid would be stupid enough to do that.

At the kitchen table, I reach for *Great Expectations*, but she stops me. "I think we'll read something else today." She shuffles across the room to a stack of shoeboxes and feels around for the right one—although I don't think there's any Braille on them. "Aha!" She smiles, her tongue clacking as she sucks on her yellowed teeth. I can't see her eyes, but her whole face sort of disappears into a mass of wrinkles. She holds up a small pamphlet and another newspaper clipping. "Read this." She looks happy and excited, but I'm not. I'm thinking of Annabel Lee, and what happened to her.

"Can we keep going on *Great Expectations*? I was really getting into Pip's story," I lie.

"Read," she insists, and I can hear all those years of being a teacher in her voice. She's still fumbling around for something else in the box, but she shoves the pamphlet into my hand, open to a page that has a picture of the Statue of Liberty on top. I read the words that are circled at the bottom of the page out loud.

"Give me your tired, your poor,
Your huddled masses yearning to breathe free,

The wretched refuse of your teeming shore.
Send these, the homeless, tempest-tossed to me . . ."

"Yes." Mrs. Carlson pulls the booklet away. "Now this."

Another page, torn from a dictionary. I can't pronounce the first word, and she sounds it out. "As-fix-ee-a. Now start again, from the beginning."

She hands me back the pamphlet. I want to ask if there's some reason I have to read it again—I didn't mess that part up, I don't think. But she's scribbling something on a piece of dirty blue paper and suddenly all I want to do is get out of there. I'll read this stuff and go. I'll tell her I'm sick.

I read the first poem again, then the definition: "Asphyxia, from the ancient Greek *a*—meaning 'without,' and *sphyxis*, meaning 'heartbeat.'" The definition is long, and it ends with "an example of asphyxia would be choking."

Not a second later, she presses the handwritten blue paper into my palm. I read fast.

"Hanging, strangling, drowned or worse,
afflict these ones with Ondine's curse.
Choke the lung and chill the blood
to nip the vandal's strangling bud."

As soon as I finish reading, I drop the paper and grab my backpack.

"Where do you think you're going?" Mrs. Carlson's black glasses reflect back two smaller versions of me, ones that look like they just witnessed something horrible. Even though nothing happened. Nothing real, anyway.

"Home," I manage. "My stomach hurts."

"Oh, really?" she says. "What sort of pain would you call it, my dear? A dull ache, or a sharp pain?" She shuffles over to her kitchen cabinet. "I have some Tums here if it's indigestion. Dull pain is usually just gas, you know. Maybe you shouldn't have the pineapple cake today."

"No," I say. "It's a sharp pain. Not gas. I think I'd better go home."

"Come back tomorrow," she calls out as I race down the street.

I spend the rest of the afternoon in bed, wondering if I'm going crazy. When I think of it, nothing Mrs. Carlson is doing should cause my heart to race, and for me to feel like . . . like she's dangerous. She's just an ex–English teacher. A widow. Her house is full of shoeboxes and newspapers, and she spends all day clipping stories out. That's all.

I get up when I hear Mom come in. By dinnertime, I can't believe the thoughts I had. Crazy stuff. Mom would probably say I'd been watching too many scary movies. Still, I feel like I should tell her something.

"I'm so glad you're spending this time with Mrs. Carlson," Mom says before I can decide how much to share. "She's all alone over there. You know, you may need help with your reading, but I have a feeling she needs you even more. I'm so proud of you."

Ugh. I definitely can't say anything now.

The next morning, Mom has the local news on while we're getting ready, and I can hear the announcer all the way in the bathroom.

"Last night around seven p.m., according to local police, two boys, residents of Round Rock, came close to dying from asphyxiation when a faulty heating unit released carbon monoxide into the living areas of the house. The boys, still in critical condition at Round Rock Hospital, are both members of the Valley View middle school football team . . ."

Valley View. My school. Max and Pedro are both on the team, and they both have brothers.

The word I learned the day before keeps swimming through my thoughts. *Asphyxia.* And other words, the ones I read out loud . . . *yearning to breathe free . . . choke the lung and chill the blood . . .*

I begin to feel like somehow I'm connected to what happened. And I start to freak out about Max and Pedro, too. Are they okay? I'm so upset, Mom drives me to school instead of making me take the bus. The principal is outside, talking to a group of parents and crying kids. I see Max and Pedro in the parking lot, and I let out the breath it feels like I've been holding since breakfast.

It's all in my imagination, I tell myself. It has nothing to do with me. It's all a coincidence.

For three days, I go back to Mrs. Carlson's, and it's *Great Expectations* for two and a half eternal hours.

By the next Monday, it's like all the stuff that happened the week before is just a bad dream. The teachers at school still cry sometimes. But Max and Pedro and I do our best not to think about it. Honestly, we're more excited about the Formula One race that's coming to Austin the next weekend. Pedro's dad is a big shot at Apple, and he's got tickets for their whole family. I try not to act jealous, even though I am.

"Hey," Pedro says. "Can you two come over today? We're going to watch the last race Dad recorded. Popcorn, pizza, ice cream. What do you say?"

"I say yes!" yells Max. They both look at me, waiting.

"I wish. I've got that stupid tutoring thing after school."

"Can you sneak away?" Pedro asks. "You can ride your bike to my house in two minutes. Stay till six thirty. Your mom doesn't even have to know."

"Right," I say. "Mom thinks Mrs. Carlson 'needs me.'"

"What does she need you for?" Pedro asks. "To gather up all the dust bunnies in her house so she can knit a granny sweater?"

"Does she need you to help her put on her adult diapers?" Max says. "You're such a dear, sweet boy. Now help an old lady put in her dentures."

He comes running at me, smacking his gums. I almost smack him in the gums with my fist.

"Don't be jerks. I hate going there." The guys must see I'm seriously bummed, because they both stop teasing me.

"Max, I think we'd better go rescue our friend today," Pedro says.

"What do you mean?" I ask, but the bell rings, and they both sprint off, and I don't see them again.

That afternoon, I'm halfway through *Great Expectations*, dying of boredom, when Mrs. Carlson puts her icy hand over mine and says, "Stop."

"What?" I'm pretty sure I didn't mess up. I'm actually reading a lot better these days. Maybe because Mrs. Carlson's black glasses make me feel like she's glaring at me whenever I miss a word, and I can never tell what she's thinking.

Clang! Bang!

Mrs. Carlson stands up, holding on to the table as she moves toward the door. I can't tell what's making the noise, but I have a sinking feeling when I hear some kids shouting. I think I recognize the voices.

"Free Jeremiah Denton!"

When I get outside the front door, I see I'm right. It's Max and Pedro, and they're beating on trash can lids with big sticks, and marching up and down in front of Mrs. Carlson's house. "Free Jeremiah Denton!" Max yells even louder when he sees us.

"Do you know these fellows?" Mrs. Carlson asks, her voice soft. She hisses on the last *s* of the word *fellows*. I suddenly imagine a snake, coiled up, ready to strike.

"Yes, ma'am," I say. "I'm sorry. I'll go ask them to stop."

"You do that. The noise is giving me a headache."

I can feel Mrs. Carlson's eyes burning holes into my back. I remind myself she probably can't see me at all this far away.

"What the heck are you two doing?" I whisper. "You're gonna get me in trouble!"

"That's her?" Pedro asks. Max is still banging on his trash can lid, like he's trying out for a band.

"Yes, and I have to go." I risk a glance behind me and see she's standing still, her head tilted to one side like she's listening.

"Whatever," Pedro says. He pitches his voice a little louder and waves for Max to stop banging. "Excuse me, ma'am? We're here for the liberation of Jeremiah Denton. Can he come to our house for a little while? It's really important."

Mrs. Carlson doesn't even shake her head. She just stares, through those dark glasses, and her lips get a little bit tighter. She looks as angry as I've ever seen her. "Leave. Now."

Max starts beating his lid again. "Let him go! Let him go! Let him go!"

Pedro joins in. "Let him go! Let him go!"

"Guys, stop!" I say. "You're going to get . . ." I almost say *hurt* but stop myself. "In trouble," I finish.

"Come on," Pedro says, "We'll wear her down." He yells for a few more seconds, then laughs. "See? She's gone back inside! That must mean she's given up. Let's go watch the race!"

"No." I look behind me. Mrs. Carlson is gone, but it feels like she's still watching. Listening. "I can't. I told you. I'll see you tomorrow."

I head for the door, and the guys yell insults at my back, and keep banging. Mrs. Carlson, at the kitchen table, is rubbing her temples.

"Fetch me that box," she says, one wrinkly hand waving toward a red shoebox on the top of a dusty stack of newspapers. My stomach feels just like it did in fourth grade when the biggest kid in school punched me in the gut because I wouldn't give up my place in the lunch line.

"Maybe we should just keep reading *Great Expectations*." My voice is weird, shaky. "I think it's really helping my reading get better. And it's a great story."

"The box," she repeats, and I feel like her covered eyes have lasers in them, mind-control lasers. I hand her the red box without meaning to. She fumbles around in it, like she really is blind, but I'm starting to have my doubts. I mean, don't blind people use canes? I'm not here all the time, but I've never seen her use a cane. She must be able to get around . . . must be able to see well enough. I don't care what my mom says, Mrs. Carlson doesn't need me. She needs something, though. An image of a straitjacket flashes in my mind.

Her lips get super tight, like she knows what I'm think-ing. "Hand me some paper now," she orders. "And a pen."

I find myself standing, carrying paper and pen from the table next to the phone and placing it in her hand.

"Thank you." Her voice is even, calm, everything I'm not feeling inside. "Now, I want you to read this first." She pushes a small booklet across the table. It's not like the other things she's asked me to read. It looks like one of those books you get from the doctor's office. The kind of thing I expect to find in an old lady's house.

I read loud enough to drown out the continued drum-ming from outside.

"The loss of thirty decibels or more of hearing ability per day is called sudden hearing loss. In most cases, sudden hearing loss affects one ear, although some sufferers experi-ence rapid hearing loss in both ears. The cause can only be found in approximately fifteen percent of cases, and can be irremediable."

I trip over the last word. "What does that mean?" I ask, my voice breathy and small.

"Unfixable," Mrs. Carlson says, and smiles. I scoot back a little in my chair. There's nothing in that booklet worth smiling about. "Now, let's finish this little task."

Task? What task does she mean? And then, I know. I've

always known. She has been doing something—using me to do something. Using me to hurt those other kids. It seems crazy, but it feels like I'm right.

But if I'm right about what has been happening, and I'm not nuts . . . what if she's not just an old lady, but something else, something evil?

The banging and chanting continues outside. What if, this time, it's Max and Pedro she's after?

I feel her cold hand on my shoulder. "Read it again, and try harder to pronounce the words correctly." Her nails feel like knives against the side of my neck as I read, slowly, stumbling. I mess up five more times, trying to give Max and Pedro time to stop, to go home.

Mrs. Carlson's nails press deeper into the side of my neck when I mess up again, this time on the word *decibels*. "You should try harder, Jeremiah. I don't want to involve your mother in this."

A chill goes through me. "You mean, you don't want to have to call my mom? About my reading."

"No," she says. "That's not what I mean."

I feel a lump of terror rise up in my throat. I read the passage correctly the next time.

She hands me another scrap of paper, with only one sentence on it. "Few love to hear the sins they love to act," I

49

read slowly. I'd heard that before. "Shakespeare?"

"Yes," she murmurs, thrusting a sheet of paper in my hand, the one she wrote. I don't look down at it.

"They didn't mean it!" The words rush out of me in a flood. I have to say something before it's too late. "They didn't mean to disturb you. They're my friends. I promise, I'll get them to quit, I'll—"

"Enough!" Mrs. Carlson says, the word dropping like a thunderclap into the sudden silence of the room. I stop talking, stop breathing. The air in the room goes cold, like a freezer door has just swung open.

"This is a reading lesson," she says finally. "Read."

My lips part without me trying, and I hear myself read her poem.

"Deaf as a beetle, deaf as a post
deaf as an adder, deaf as a ghost
resound, reverberate, rumble, roar
tinnitus profundus will vex evermore."

I'm going to be sick. I have to go warn my friends. I have to leave. "My stomach," I say, pulling away. "I've got to go to the bathroom."

"Down the hall," she says. "Sharp pains again?"

"Yes, really sharp. I've gotta go home."

She follows me to the front door, faster than any woman who is supposed to be blind should be able to move. "Come back tomorrow," she calls after me, "and I'll make you a special batch of cookies to help with that stomachache. We're not done with our lessons."

Yes we are, I think, racing for my front door. I don't think I'm going to read anything, ever again. I fumble for my key, and slam the door shut behind me.

I get online and look up the word *tinnitus*. A ringing in the ears? That doesn't sound too bad.

But the next day, I'm in the cafeteria when Max and Pedro get to school. Max keeps shaking his head, hard, like he's trying to shake something loose.

"What's up, Max?" He shrugs and sits next to me. Pedro joins him, holding his head like he has a headache.

"It's probably good you didn't come over last night. I think I'm getting sick," Pedro says. "My ears are ringing."

I go cold all over.

"Me too," Max says, rubbing his temples. "It keeps getting louder. My mom says she'll take me to the doctor if it gets worse."

It's happening. I have to tell someone what I suspect about Mrs. Carlson. Even if they don't believe me. I have to try.

"Guys . . . ," I start, but then the morning bell for classes goes off. And goes on, longer and longer, louder and louder. Everyone in the cafeteria starts shouting. "What's happening? There's a malfunction!" People are covering their ears, and I am, too—until I notice Max has fallen to the floor and is rolling there, holding the sides of his head, crying. Pedro falls down a few seconds later, and I see something seeping through his hair and between his fingers. Blood?

I grab their arms and race them to the school nurse, away from the cafeteria speaker. I sit with them while they cry, while their parents are called. "You can go back to your first period class," the nurse says, patting me on the shoulder. "They'll be all right," she adds, but she doesn't look certain.

"What happened?"

The nurse frowns. "I'm not sure. From what I could see, their eardrums burst. But it's very unusual for that to happen so quickly, and all four—" She breaks off. "Go back to class, Jeremiah."

I am sick now, sick with guilt. I did this. Or, I helped Mrs. Carlson do . . . whatever she did.

I can't go back.

That day, I stay in my room. I don't answer the phone, even though it rings over and over. I don't answer the doorbell. I don't even turn on a light, in case Mrs. Carlson is watching.

But that means when Mom gets back from work, she doesn't know I'm home either. Too late to stop her, I watch from my window as she goes down the street to Mrs. Carlson's house, looking for me.

Ten minutes later, Mom is at my door, a frown on her face. "What's wrong?"

I can't tell her. But I start crying, begging Mom not to make me go back. When she asks why, I just say, "I can't. I can't do it anymore."

To my surprise, Mom sighs and nods. "I think you might be getting sick. I haven't seen you so upset since you were a toddler with the flu. It's probably best not to expose Mrs. Carlson to germs anyway. Old people have fragile immune systems. I'll explain to her."

By Friday, Mom says I'm well enough to go back to Mrs. Carlson's, but for the first time in a week, I'm not worried. I hand Mom my report card.

"What? An A! In English! You have to tell Mrs. Carlson!"

"But . . . I'm done, right? I don't have to do any more lessons, do I?"

Mom looks disappointed. "Well . . . I guess not. I did say you could stop when you got your grades up. But don't you think you might, just to keep her company? Maybe not every day . . ."

"No, never again," I say, managing to keep my voice from shaking. "I'm done."

Mom frowns. "Well, you have to go over at least once more to say thank you, and show her your report card."

"Sure, Mom," I lie. "I'll go in a little while."

I've never been a very good liar. Mom suspects something. "Go now," she says, and watches me walk all the way to Mrs. Carlson's house.

Before I even finish ringing the doorbell, she's there. Like she's been waiting, like she knew I was coming. "Ah, Jeremiah," she says, pushing the screen door open. "Come in. I need you to read something special for me today."

"No," I say, stepping back. "I'm done." I show her my report card.

"Just read one more thing," she insists. "I'll give you something special once you do." She reaches behind her, then thrusts a hand toward me, a hand full of what look like tiny wiggling snakes, or worms. I jump back, away from the disgusting things, and the screen door slaps against her hand. "Ouch!" She cradles her hand to her chest. "You hurt me."

"I'm s-sorry," I stammer, realizing what I thought was

snakes is just more of her weird licorice. But I could swear it had moved. Her hands must have been shaking. "I'm sorry," I repeat, running away from her dark glasses, her searching hands, her angry, pinched face.

I can't sleep at all; I keep hearing her accusing me, "You hurt me."

The next two weeks, I go straight to Max's or Pedro's after school, helping them catch up on their missed homework. They're both deaf, but the doctors are hoping surgery will help. If not, they might have to go to a different school, one for deaf kids.

Guilt eats at me every day. Bringing them their assignments is the least I can do. I can't tell them what I think really happened. I sure can't tell them what part I played in it. I can't forgive myself, though. I'll never be able to.

And I still can't sleep. I dream of Mrs. Carlson at my door, at my window, holding out a bleeding hand full of dark candy, forcing me to read mysterious handwritten poems about myself, about my mom.

But after two months pass, the nightmares fade, and I realize it's all over. She hasn't called or come by. And aside from the occasional stomachaches I get, my mom and I are both fine.

I practice my reading every single night for an hour or more anyway, never taking a day off.

Then one day, on my way home from Max's, I see someone coming out of Mrs. Carlson's house. A kid, a little younger than me. He's chewing on something, and stuffing a paper in his pocket. I wait until he gets on his bike and comes down the street before I wave to get his attention.

"Hey, kid! What were you doing in there?"

He parks his bike. "Hanging out with a crazy old lady," he says. "It's, like, a part-time job I got."

"A job doing what?"

"You'd never guess. Reading!"

I peek down at Mrs. Carlson's front window and see the curtain twitch, like she's watching. I pull the kid toward me and whisper. "Listen, dude, I don't know how much she's paying you, but it's not worth it. She's messed up."

He pulls his arm away. "I know that! I mean, I get twenty bucks for a half an hour's work. But today, I got the money after, like, three minutes."

Three minutes? "What did you read?"

Suddenly, a pain travels up from under my ribs, near my stomach. Like a knife is ripping at my guts, slowly tearing through them. Am I sick?

"Three random things," he says, swinging his leg back over his bike, eager to go. "She dug 'em out of shoeboxes. Well, two of them anyway."

"Random things? What things?" At that instant, I feel something inside me, something sharp and cold and more painful than anything I've ever felt.

"It was sort of gross, you know. But old ladies are gross. They smell weird." He set his foot on the pedal.

"Just tell me," I manage to gasp. "What did she have you read?" Who was she after this time? Who was going to end up at the hospital before they went home again? *If* they ever went home again?

And then, when another knife tears through my gut, I know.

"Dude, are you okay?" The kid reaches out, lays his hand on my shoulder. I almost fall down; it makes the pain double in my stomach. "You look really sick. Are you gonna hurl?"

"No," I say, trying to speak normally. "I just—tell me, okay? Please."

"Well, first she had me read a candy wrapper."

"What candy wrapper?"

"It was the ingredients on some licorice she'd just given to me."

The pains in my stomach get more intense . . . and suddenly it feels like it's . . . moving. Up my esophagus, out through the walls of my stomach, down to my intestines.

"What else," I pant, leaning down, trying to catch my breath.

"Something about industrial-grade steel," he says. He's on his bike now, riding around me, and I can't make out all the words, but I think I hear, "Like, how to make it? It was really confusing. There were some tricky words in that part for sure."

"And then what?" I gasp, but I think I know. In fact, I'm almost sure what she wrote. Because I look down at my stomach and I can see—

"It was a poem!" His words interrupt my thoughts, the horror of what I realize is happening. "A really short one. I have it here."

He pulls the paper out of his pocket with one hand. *"Thankless bite, silver bright, flesh to steel, now reveal.* Weird, right? She said it was a poem she wrote for some kid who took her candy and slammed the door on her. Crazy old lady, like I said."

He rides off then, trailing the smell of licorice. I keep my feet until he turns the corner, and then I fall to the ground. All I can feel is pain, sharp pain, like I have a stomach full of glass.

No, not glass. I look down and see a tiny glint in the sunlight. One pinprick of bright metal, flashing silver and red. I pull on it, pull it out of my skin, out of my stomach, feeling the hundreds of other spots where the skin is beginning to bulge and pucker.

In my hand I hold a needle.

THE BLUE-BEARDED
BIRD-MAN
BY ADAM GIDWITZ

Once upon a ti—

I'll stop. You don't even want me to finish that sentence. Now you think I'm going to tell you a *fairy tale*. You did not pick up this book in order to read a fairy tale. You picked up this book to read a story that would scare you; that would freak you out; that would give you nightmares; a story so scary you'd pee in your pants. *That's* the kind of story you're looking for. Right?

Well, you're in luck. I'm going to tell you the scariest, bloodiest, most messed-up story I have ever heard. It will probably make you pee in your pants.

It also happens to be a fairy tale.
So go get an extra pair of pants. You're gonna need them.

Once upon a time, deep in a great, wild wood, there lived three brothers and three sisters.

The three brothers were all fine hunters, while the three sisters were all very beautiful—all except the youngest sister, who was rather plain. Still, she was the bravest and cleverest of them all. Her name was Marleen, but because she was the littlest, they called her Marleenken, which means "little Marlene."

Wait a minute . . . Now you're probably thinking that this story is going to be about somebody's annoying little sister. This book is called *Guys Read: Terrifying Tales*. Not *Guys Read: Annoying Little Sisters*. And especially not *Guys Read: Fairy Tales About Annoying Little Sisters*.

Anyway, yes, you're going to read about someone's little sister. And you're going to like it.

The only other person who lived in the great, wild wood was a recluse, a crazy man, a real weirdo. He was a fowler—a bird-catcher. He set sharp wire traps all over the forest, and he would go from trap to trap, collecting the birds that had been caught in them, wringing their necks, and shoving them in his great, big basket. The fowler had wide, bulging eyes and a long beard so black it was almost blue.

None of the three brothers or three sisters knew where he lived, except that it was somewhere in the great, wild wood.

One day, while the three brothers were out hunting, and Marleenken was sitting by her window, daydreaming, she saw a very strange sight.

Her eldest sister was getting water from the well. But as she leaned over to pull up the bucket, the fowler crept out of the woods. He had his big bird-catching basket on his back, and his blue beard shimmered in the morning light. He tiptoed up behind Marleenken's eldest sister and grabbed her and threw her in his basket. Then he ran away.

Marleenken screamed, ran from the house, and tried to see where he had gone. But he had disappeared, like a bird at the sound of a gunshot. She went to her second sister and told her what had happened. But her second sister didn't believe her. It was too strange.

Later, when her three brothers came home from hunting, Marleenken told them what she had seen. They didn't believe her either. "Where is my eldest sister, then?" she demanded.

"She'll be back soon, I'm sure," said her oldest brother.

He seems very concerned, doesn't he? Way to look out for your siblings, dude.

To Marleenken's great surprise, though, her sister *was* home soon. That night, at the very moment when the sun was setting and the moon was rising, Marleenken's eldest sister walked into the clearing where their little house stood. All her brothers and sisters ran up to her to greet her. She smiled at them and told them that the most wonderful thing had happened. She had married the fowler, and she would live in his great house and be rich and happy for the rest of her life.

Okay, kids. Life-lesson time.

There are some good ways to propose marriage: You can get down on one knee; you can buy a fancy ring; you can take a trip to a tropical island; you can go to Paris. Any of those are great. You should absolutely try one of those.

There are also some *bad* ways to propose marriage. These include throwing your sweetheart into a basket and running away with her.

**That's pretty much the *worst* way to propose.
Just so you know.**

Marleenken and her brothers and sisters were all very confused. They had not known that the fowler was rich. And they were surprised that they had not been invited to the wedding. But their sister seemed happy, so they were, too. All except for Marleenken. Marleenken knew what she had seen. She did not trust the blue-bearded fowler. No. He frightened her.

Marleenken's eldest sister spent one last night with her family in their little house, and then she waved good-bye to Marleenken and her brothers and the second sister and left for the fowler's again.

The eldest sister had not lied. His house was very grand indeed. When she returned to it, he was all courtesy, smiling and bowing and kissing her hand. Then he gave her a set of keys. "These keys open any door in the house," he said. "You may go anywhere you like. Except do not go in the little door at the end of the hall." He held up a tiny golden key. "If you go in that door, I will be very, very angry." Finally, he gave her an egg, as blue and delicate as a robin's. "Keep this egg with you," he said. "If you can keep it clean, I will know that you love me, and we shall be happy together for as long as you live." The girl agreed. He seemed like a very nice man.

The first time the fowler left the house, the girl set out to explore every inch of it. Holding the keys in her right hand and the egg in her left, she went from room to room. Never had she seen such a splendid house. The fowler must have been very rich indeed.

But when she had seen every single room, cupboard, and closet, she wanted to see more. She looked at the little door at the end of the hall. She looked at the tiny golden key. She went to the front of the house and peered out, to make sure that the fowler wasn't about to come home. Then she hurried back to the door and put the key in the keyhole.

The lock turned with a slow *click*.

The door slowly swung open.

The girl screamed.

I told you this was going to be scary, right? And bloody? And messed up? I wasn't lying.

If you've changed your mind, and you don't want to read something scary and bloody and messed up, I won't blame you at all. No sweat. Just go ahead and turn to the next story in this book. I think it's called "Annoying Little Sisters—A Fairy Tale."

No? You're still reading? Okay. Don't say I didn't warn you.

From the ceiling hung sacks. Big, bloody sacks. Dozens of them. The girl could hear the slow, syncopated drip of blood from the sacks onto the floor.

In the middle of the room stood a great basin, filled with blood. She walked up to the basin. In it, a blue egg bobbed. The girl looked to her hand. She wasn't carrying her egg anymore. She must have thrown it in the air when she screamed. Now it had fallen in the basin. She snatched the egg from the blood and tried to wipe it clean—but it would not get clean. A nasty red stain spread over the delicate blue shell.

And then she heard the front door open.

She ran to the door of the bloody room. Where were her keys? Where were her keys? She looked down. She had dropped them. She retrieved them from the floor. The tiny golden key was sticky with blood. She tried to wipe it off— but the red stain would not go away.

Footsteps echoed in the hallway. She slipped out of the room, closed the door behind her, and put her back against it.

And then she saw the fowler. He was grinning at her.

"Hello, my dear," he said.

She could not speak.

"Have you had a nice time in my absence?"

She had no breath.

"Did you keep the egg nice and clean, like I asked you to?"
She could not even move her head to nod.

"Let me see it," he said.

She could not resist him. She did not know why, but she could not. She held out the egg.

The blood had spread all over it, making it mottled, grotesque, and purple.

The fowler looked sad. "And where, my dear, is the little golden key?"

Again, the girl could not resist. She held up the key. It was sticky and red with blood.

The fowler sighed. Then he smiled. "You have gone into my private room once. You shall go in once more—and never come out again."

He reached into his basket and took out an axe.
And he used it.

Are we okay out there? Probably not. I have had to change my pants twice now while telling this story.

Don't worry, though. It doesn't get worse than that.

Of course, it doesn't get *better* either.

A few days later, when the three brothers were out hunting, and Marleenken was sitting at her little window, she saw her second sister drawing water from the well. But as her sister leaned over to pull up the bucket, the fowler crept out of the woods. He had his big bird-catching basket on his back, and his blue beard shimmered in the morning light. He tiptoed up behind Marleenken's second sister and grabbed her and threw her in his basket. Then he ran away.

Marleenken did not scream this time, but she did run from the house to see where he had gone. Again, he had disappeared, like a bird at the sound of an axe against a tree.

When her brothers came home from hunting, Marleenken told them what she had seen. Again, they didn't believe her. "Where is my second sister, then?" she demanded.

"She'll be back soon, I'm sure," said her oldest brother.

Sure enough, she was. That night, at the very moment when the sun was setting and the moon was rising, Marleenken's second sister walked into the clearing where their little house stood. All her brothers ran up to her to greet her. Marleenken did not. The sister smiled at them and told them that the most wonderful thing had happened. She had married the fowler, and she would live in his great house and be rich and happy for the rest of her life.

"Wait!" Marleenken cried. "What happened to our oldest sister, then?"

"Oh, she went away. The fool! His house is so grand, and his manners are so fine!"

Marleenken's second sister spent one last night with her family in their little house, and then she left for the fowler's.

Again, the fowler gave the sister a pretty blue egg and a ring of keys, and again he told her to keep the egg clean, and that she could look in any door in the house except the little door at the end of the hall. And he left.

Soon, the second sister had seen every room in the house, except for the one at the end of the hall. She tried and tried and tried to resist, but her curiosity was too strong. Finally, she took the little golden key between her fingers and opened the little door.

The lock turned with a slow *click*.

The door slowly swung open.

The girl screamed.

She, too, saw the floor covered with thick, sticky blood.

She saw the sacks, bloody and ever so slightly swaying from the ceiling.

And in the middle of the room she saw the basin, filled with blood. Bobbing in the blood was her egg.

And also, her sister. Well, pieces of her sister.

She screamed and dropped the key.

Soon, the fowler came home. The axe came out. And the girl went into the room one last time.

Okay, have you had to change your pants yet?
Personally, I had to go to the store and buy a few more
pairs. That's how I'm doing.

Now, when her brothers went out hunting, Marleenken did not have time to sit by the window and daydream. She had to do all the chores that her sisters used to do. Including fetching water from the well. But whenever she did this, she took a little mirror with her, and set it on the edge of the well.

One day, as she leaned down into the well to draw up the bucket, she spied, in the little mirror, a figure emerging from the woods. Marleenken watched as it moved through the shade of the trees. Finally, it stepped into the sun. It was the Blue-Bearded Bird-Man, with his fowling basket over his shoulder. He tiptoed up behind her.

Suddenly, Marleenken spun around. "What are you doing here?" she demanded.

The fowler was startled. He stammered a bit. Then he said, "I have come to ask you to be my wife."

"What about my sister? Isn't she your wife?"

"She went away," said the fowler. He did not look Marleenken in the eye.

"Okay," Marleenken said. "But I'm not getting in that basket. If you want me to be your wife, you have to let me walk to your house beside you."

The Blue-Bearded Bird-Man grinned. His teeth were rotten. "Oh! Anything you say, my dear!" And he led the way through the forest to his house.

The house was big and old and beautiful, and the fowler was all courtesy, just as he had been with Marleenken's sisters—smiling and bowing and kissing her hand. He gave her the keys and said, "These keys open any door in the house. You may go anywhere you like. Except do not go in the little door at the end of the hall." He held up a tiny golden key. "If you go in that door, I will be very, very angry." And then he gave her the egg, delicate and blue as a robin's. "Keep this egg with you," he said. "If you can keep it clean, I will know that you love me, and we shall be happy together for as long as you live."

Marleenken looked at the egg. "What's so special about it?" she asked.

The fowler looked confused. "Nothing. I just want you to hold on to it."

"Well, then I don't want it," Marleenken replied, and she

handed it back to him.

The fowler frowned. "Fine," he said. "If you want to know the truth, it is a magical egg. Now, don't ask me any more questions, or I shall be very angry indeed."

Marleenken nodded and took the egg back.

"Now, I am leaving you alone for a while. Remember what I've told you."

"Don't worry," said Marleenken. "I'll remember."

Marleenken watched from the window as the Blue-Bearded Bird-Man disappeared into the forest. As soon as he was out of sight, she started to search the house for her sisters, for she did not believe that they had just gone away. She went in every room in the house, but she could not find them anywhere. At last, she came to the little door at the end of the hall. She glanced at the door. She glanced at her egg. She put the egg in a big pocket of her dress. "Who knows what's behind that door?" she said. "Maybe the bird that laid this egg. Best to keep it safe." Then she put the tiny golden key in the keyhole and unlocked the door. She removed the key from the keyhole and put it in her pocket. Finally, very slowly, she pushed the door open.

She gasped, but she did not scream.

She saw the blood, lying thick and sticky on the floor.

She saw the bags, swaying, swaying, swaying from the ceiling.

And she saw the basin of blood, and in the basin, she saw her sisters, all chopped up into pieces.

Hanging from the ceiling just above the fountain, she saw empty bags . . . one, two, three of them.

She closed the little door behind her. She walked to the basin across the sticky, bloody floor. She took her sisters out of the basin—an arm here, a leg here, now an eyeball, now an ear.

She laid her sisters' body parts on the bloody floor, putting each one where it was supposed to be. Then she took the egg from her pocket, cracked the egg, and rubbed the bright orange yolk all over her hands. Finally, she smeared her sisters with the egg. As the yolk touched their corpses, the pieces of them magically grew back together. Finally, she put the eggshells on their eyes—first on her oldest sister's eyes, then on her second sister's eyes. And one by one, the girls came back to life.

WHAT? How did that happen? That makes no sense.

I know. I agree. But it's a *fairy tale*. Fairy tales aren't supposed to make sense. They're supposed to scare the bejeezus out of you.

On that count, I think we're doing okay. Don't you?

The sisters stood up and looked around. Just then, they heard the front door open.

"Shhh!" Marleenken said. "Stay here, and don't make a sound!" And she slipped out of the little door, locked it with the key behind her, and went to greet the Blue-Bearded Bird-Man.

"Well, my little wife," he said. "How did you pass the time?"

"I explored every room in the house."

"And did you open the little door at the end of the hall?"

"Of course not. You told me I couldn't."

"Then let me see the key."

So Marleenken showed him the key. Having been in her pocket the whole time she was in the room, it was as clean and golden as ever.

"Very good," he said. Then he paused, and smiled with his bulging eyes and blue beard. "Now, show me the egg."

Do you know what's going to happen now? Are you scared? I know I am.

Marleenken drew the two halves of the eggshell from her pocket.

"What have you done?" the fowler shouted. "That is the last mistake you shall ever make!" And he reached for the axe in his basket.

"Why, dear husband?" Marleenken said. "You told me that I had to keep the egg clean! It is very clean!"

"But where are its insides?"

"I got hungry, so I ate them," said Marleenken.

The Blue-Bearded Bird-Man stared at her over his long, beak-like beard. "Hm," he said. And then he said it again. "Hm."

"Oh," said Marleenken, as if it were an afterthought. "I got a letter from my brothers while you were out."

"What? How do they know where I live?"

"Well, I wrote to them first," said Marleenken.

If I were the fowler, I would have asked, "Wait, since when is there a postal service in the great, wild wood? And how does it work so fast?"

Luckily, though, he didn't think of that.

He merely asked, "What did the letter say?"

"It said that they suspect you of killing my sisters."

"WHAT?" The fowler's bulging eyes nearly burst from his head.

"I know it isn't true. But they think my sisters' bodies are here in this house."

"WHAT?" The fowler began biting his lips until they were as blue as his beard.

"I know it isn't true. But they said they're coming here this very day to kill you."

"WHAT?" The fowler had begun to tremble like a bird in a trap.

"I think that part is true. And they are very great hunters. I would be worried if I were you."

"What can we do?" the fowler bawled. "Whatever can we do?"

"I've been thinking about that," said Marleenken. "I could tell them not to kill you, but I don't think they'll listen to me."

"So what can we do? Whatever can we do?"

"You could hide somewhere in the house, but I'm pretty sure they would find you and kill you."

"So what can we do? Whatever can we do?"

"I came up with a plan."

"Tell me! Tell me! Save me, dearest Marleenken!"

"I think you should cover yourself in honey."

"WHAT?"

"And then cover yourself in feathers."

"WHAT?"

"And I think you should sneak into the forest. You will look just like a bird, with your big blue beard as a beak, and you can hide there until my brothers go away."

The fowler stared down at Marleenken with his bulging eyes. His arms twitched. Marleenken suddenly wondered if he was going to kill her. But then he said, "I have honey in the kitchen."

So Marleenken helped the Blue-Bearded Bird-Man cover himself in honey, and then she cut open one of his great feather mattresses and dumped the feathers all over him. And he did, indeed, look just like an enormous, blue-beaked bird. He thanked Marleenken for being so clever, and he ran out into the forest.

Marleenken watched until he was out of sight. Then she went to the little door at the end of the hall and opened it. "Come quick!" she said. "Now we go home!"

So she and her sisters hurried from the house and into the forest.

But as they made their way home, they heard something in the trees.

"What's that?" her eldest sister asked.

Marleenken did not know. They went faster.

"I hear something behind us," said the second sister.

Marleenken made them hurry even more.

And then, through the trees, Marleenken saw him. His eyes were wide and insane. His feathers shone in the darkness like mist. His blue beard glowed like the flame at the center of a fire. And he hefted his great, bloody axe above his head.

"RUN!" Marleenken screamed.

The sisters ran, and the Blue-Bearded Bird-Man ran after them. They ran, but the Bird-Man ran faster. Soon, he was right behind them. He swung his axe.

The forest echoed like a gunshot. Marleenken kept running. At last, she glanced behind her. Her sisters were panting and gasping, but they were right there with her.

They arrived at the house. They burst through their door and slammed it behind them.

They waited.

A few hours later, their brothers came home. The boys were thrilled to see all three of their sisters back again. They laughed and hugged one another and fought back tears.

"We saw the strangest thing in the forest today," said the oldest brother. "It was the biggest bird we'd ever seen. It was white like the fog, with a giant blue beak."

"What happened?" asked Marleenken.

Do you know what happened? Do you have a guess?

Her oldest brother smiled. "What do you think happened? We're hunters. We shot it."

Marleenken sighed. "Oh," she said. "That's good."

And the three brothers and the three sisters lived happily ever after.

THE END

DON'T EAT THE BABY
BY KELLY BARNHILL

Before I start this story, let me first say that it is never, never, never, never, *never* okay to push your brother down a creepy, old, possibly bottomless well.

Or, *almost never.*

Let me tell you something else, too. I am a scout. My best friend, Jamal, is also a scout. We can both start fires without matches, and can find our way with a map and compass, and can communicate with Morse Code and, by last count, are able to tie forty-six different types of knots correctly, while blindfolded. I am telling you this not to brag—even though it *is* pretty cool—but because it is important for later.

Also, because everyone should know Morse Code. And knots. That's just common sense.

* * *

My whole life, I wanted a brother. And I never had one until last Tuesday. Instead, I had a very annoying baby sister. I also had two rats, four rabbits, seven fish, one canary, three guinea pigs, one salamander, and one very fat, very old, and very mean cat named Owen—but I never really counted him because he is way older than me. Plus, he belongs to my mom.

I've always been in charge of my animals. My mom doesn't do a thing. Except for the cat, of course. I clean the cages and scrub the bowls and check their paws and fill their water and make sure they have the right foods. I make lists every Monday for my mom, telling her what to buy. My dad calls me the Family Caretaker. My mom calls me Zookeeper Arne. My sister doesn't call me anything. Except *Boy*. She just sits in her high chair, shoveling OatieBits into her mouth and grinding her teeth like she's sharpening them. They gleam like blades.

I always wanted a brother. Not a boring baby sister. Sometimes, I'd ask Mom if I could have one, but she was always cleaning OatieBits from the walls or ceiling or mopping up Owen's most recent furball. Each time she'd just stare at me, as though I had suddenly appeared out of nowhere, or like I was speaking another language. And then she'd shake her head and say, "Don't you have a cage to clean or something?" And she'd walk away.

And whatever. She was usually right. But that's not the point.

I *really wanted* a brother. Not a fish. Not a lizard. Not a rat. A brother. Who would ride bikes with me and play Monopoly and do experiments in the kitchen.

Mom used to do experiments in the kitchen with me. But now she is too busy with my dumb sister.

Dad used to play Monopoly. But now he has this new job and he doesn't get home until late, and when he does, he's tired and in a bad mood.

So I decided to take drastic action.

I brought Jamal with me. In addition to being my best friend, he lives next door, and he is in my class. He is ten months older than I am, but I am way taller. He doesn't have any pets, but he does have a microscope, which *would* have made us even. But it didn't. Because Jamal had something else, too.

Brothers. Four of them. It wasn't fair.

"Why do you *want* a brother, anyway?" Jamal asked as we climbed through the gap at the bottom of the fence that marked the end of the subdivision and the beginning of the unbuildable land. There was a trail back there that most people can't see. You can find it only if you know where to look.

Jamal and I have been back there, like, a million times, even though we aren't supposed to. Mom says the dirt is toxic and my dad says there's sinkholes and quickmud, and Jamal's mom says there are criminals living in tents, and Jamal's dad says there is a bunch of old tools and equipment back there that could possibly cut off our fingers and then Jamal will never be a surgeon. All of those things are true, but we have been okay so far.

"Brothers are not that great," Jamal continued as we scrambled under the fence, scraping our bellies on the ground. "They steal your stuff and make fun of you and play too rough. Plus? They stink." This was for sure true for Jamal's oldest brother, who was a wrestler on the high school squad. He had B.O. even if he had only just gotten out of the shower. Also, it was true of his youngest brother, who was still in diapers and could stop a herd of elephants with one whiff from his butt.

"I just want one. Is that a crime?" I said, brushing the grass and gravel off my knees. I couldn't explain *why* I wanted a brother, only that I *did*.

"Meow," Owen said in a sniffy voice. Owen always followed us when we went into the unbuildable land. I don't know how he always knew. We used to try and chase him off, but he always came back, every single time. And even when we tried to throw him off our trail, he always found us again. Now we just tolerate him.

Our subdivision is on something called a Superfund site, which makes it sound like it has superpowers, but it doesn't. My dad said it means the land used to be polluted, but now it has been cleaned up. And then they built houses. The unbuildable land is a Superfund site too, only it hasn't been cleaned yet. For some reason, everything goes wrong when they try. The money dries up. Or they find historical artifacts, and they have to stop. Or weird disasters strike. Once, a rain cloud hovered over only the unbuildable land and dumped water for hours, flooding *only there* and nowhere else. My dad said there had been several different factories going way back to the early days, and each one of them had some sort of major mishap and collapsed, leaking gross stuff all over the place, which meant that the ground was even more polluted than other Superfund sites. The most recent factory had been dismantled and cleared out years ago, leaving only a large tangle of sumac bushes and some dead cottonwood trees. And right by the factory site, there was a well.

A very, very old well.

I don't think any of the adults in the subdivision knew about it—otherwise, I'm sure there would have been some mom gathering signatures to get it filled in. Parents in our neighborhood are nuts about safety.

The well was hidden by a ring of falling-down trees. You had to climb over old, rotting branches just to get to it.

And it was haunted. Or magic. Or both. Everyone said so.

The kids in the neighborhood will swear up and down that if you make a wish, and throw your wish into the well, it gets granted. Somehow. Some way. Every single time. All you have to do is write it on a piece of paper, tie it to a rock, and send it down.

The well is deep. So deep that no one has ever heard the rock hit the bottom. And it smells bad. And there is a weird wind that comes up through the hole all the time, like it is constantly exhaling.

Some kids think it's dangerous. But they are the ones who haven't made wishes.

I reach in and grab a rock from my pocket.

"What do you think you're doing?" Jamal said.

"What does it look like?" I said, wrapping my note around the rock and tying it tight with a timber hitch. (I didn't even have to look. The knot was perfect. I'm that good.)

I'd never made a wish before. Neither had Jamal. I didn't

want to admit it, but the hairs on my arms were standing straight up. I told myself it was because it was cold. Even though it wasn't actually cold.

"It never goes right," Jamal said. "Ask anyone."

"You don't know anyone who actually *made* a wish." Which was true. We knew that kids in the subdivision had done it, but we didn't know *which ones*. So we didn't know how it all turned out.

"My brother says you can't undo it," Jamal said. "Even if you want to. There's no take-backs with wishes."

"Did he make a wish?"

"No." Jamal crossed his arms across his chest. "He never would."

"Well then. Sounds like he doesn't know what he's talking about."

I walked up to the edge of the well. The wind coming from the dark depths seemed to be picking up speed. I held out the rock.

Jamal grabbed my forearm. "Don't do it," he said, his eyes suddenly big. "It's too scary."

But I flicked my wrist and let it fly. It hit the far side of the well once with a loud thud, then plunged silently into the darkness. Owen arched his back. His fur became prickly and tall. He began to yowl.

* * *

That was Friday.

That night, I had a weird dream. I dreamed I was walking on a long, straight road. It plunged into one side of the sky at one end, and the other side of the sky at the other. My steps crunched on the pavement.

"Hello!" I called.

"I'm right here," a voice whispered in my year. I whipped around, but no one was there.

"Hello!" I called again. I was starting to panic.

"Still here," the voice whispered in the other ear.

No one was there. I was alone on the road.

I woke up, panting and sweaty. My room was empty, save for the fish, lizard, guinea pigs, rabbits, and bird. And yet. I couldn't shake the feeling that someone else was there too.

I could hear Owen hissing in the hallway.

"Crazy cat," I muttered. *Crazy me*, I thought. And I went back to sleep.

On Saturday, my mom was annoyed. The salt was gone. All of it. From the shakers, from the canister. Even the big bag of salt she keeps on the porch for the next time the sky decides to throw ice and snow at us.

"Well, what on earth?" Mom said, mystified.

"We must have run out yesterday," Dad said as he typed an email to his boss on his laptop while simultaneously shoveling eggs and toast and coffee into his mouth. Sometimes it seems like my dad has six hands.

"I didn't think we did," Mom said, scratching her head.

"I don't see any other explanation," Dad said. "By the way, these eggs would be better with salt on them."

On Sunday, my dad's laptop caught fire. Right in the middle of an email. Which he was writing at the dinner table. Which is super not allowed.

"You see?" Mom said calmly, as if spontaneously-combusting laptops were an everyday thing in our house. "This is why it's not allowed."

"GET SOMETHING TO SMOTHER IT!" Dad screamed.

Everything on it was lost. Even the keys melted.

"Bad luck," Mom said, but it didn't sound like she meant it. Nothing made her madder than my dad using technology at the dinner table.

Later that night, the television shattered. No one was in the room. This time, my mom *and* my dad seemed mystified.

Meanwhile, Owen the cat howled and hissed and whined. He ran into my parents' room and jammed himself under their bed, refusing to come out.

On Monday, my rats vanished. Without a trace. I blamed Owen.

"He ate them!" I shouted. "He ate Jeeves and Bertie! I HATE THAT CAT!"

"Owen did no such thing," my mom soothed. "He's been under my bed this whole time. You are making a fuss over nothing. Your rats are probably just exploring the house. They'll be back before you know it, I'm sure of it."

"You know," my dad said. "It is almost Halloween. We might have ghosts. If there's one thing a rat won't abide, it's a ghost. They'll leave as soon as a house is haunted."

"How do you know?" I demanded.

My dad shrugged. "Everyone knows that. If you want to get rid of rats, get a ghost. Common knowledge."

"But what if I want my rats to come back?"

Dad frowned. "I guess you have to get rid of the ghost."

But it wasn't a ghost at all. It was a brother.

He showed up the next day, after I had been having the weirdest dream. I saw a pair of hands holding a book called

Excellent Recipes for the Average Family, and it showed cut-out silhouettes of a mom, a dad, a boy, a girl, and a cat all standing in a roasting pan with a question mark on it. The person put the book down and I could see his face. It was my face.

I woke up with a yelp.

"Can it, will ya?" a voice said. "I'm trying to sleep."

I lay in bed for a full minute, trying to decide if the voice was real or not. I turned on the light.

"It's the middle of the night," the voice complained. It was coming from under my bed. "Turn off the light!"

I took a deep breath and peeked. And there he was. My brother. Lying there with my old, mismatched socks and broken toys and other stuff that I never really wanted in the first place. He was examining the springs under my mattress, tap, tap, tapping the old metal with his fingernails. He was obviously my brother. I knew without being told.

"Hey, brother," he said.

"Hey, brother," I said. My wish! The well worked. *I knew it.*

I crawled down onto the floor. I stared at him. He looked just like me. We had the same weird swoop in our hair that won't stay down no matter how many times you comb it. He was wearing the same striped pj's. He even had the same smudge of dirt on his cheek that my mom had bugged me about but I hadn't washed yet.

"How long have you been here?" I asked.

"Dunno." He yawned and waved his hand toward the bedside table. "Turn off the light, will you? I'm tired." He rolled onto his side and curled away from me, his back curved like a turtle's shell. I checked the clock. Three o'clock in the morning. I clicked off the light and went back to sleep. I didn't dream. I only heard a cat howling over and over and over.

I have a brother, I thought, my heart growing bigger and bigger. *I have a brother!* I was so happy, I could hardly stand it.

I didn't see my brother when I woke up the next morning. My mom hollered that I needed to get up, so I grabbed my clothes and stumbled into the bathroom. When I got back, my brother was there, wearing the exact same clothes as I was. He wrinkled his mouth like a prune.

"Are you hungry?" I asked.

"Not yet," he said. "But my mouth is all salty. Do you have any water?" He looked around the room. "Never mind. I see some." And before I could stop him, he plunged his face into my fish tank and started sucking the water down. *He wasn't kidding,* I thought. My fish dove for cover under the little castle my dad and I had made out of mortar and rocks.

"Stop!" I said, but he didn't stop. *"Stop,"* I said again, and grabbed him by the back of the shirt and pulled him up. The tank was only half-full now. His face—my face—was dripping wet.

"Fine!" he said. Maybe I was being unreasonable. He hadn't been in the house for very long. How was he to know what was allowed and what wasn't?

"Here," I said. "Drink from this glass." I gave him the water glass I was drinking from the night before. I figured, if we were brothers, we had the same germs. He drank it like he was dying of thirst.

I glanced at the clock. I needed to eat my breakfast and get to school. "You coming down?" I asked.

"Nah," my brother said. "Mom's not ready yet. She's delicate."

"Oh. Okay," I said. "I could bring something up. You hungry?"

"No," he said. "I just ate." He coughed and something yellow flew out of his mouth. Like a piece of paper. Or a feather.

When I got home later that day, I realized that my canary was missing. My brother told me the cat did it. Of course I believed him. He's my brother. Why would he lie? In a huff, I marched to my parents' room and fished Owen out from under the bed and carried him, hissing and spitting, outside.

"Bad kitty!" I scolded.

"Meow," Owen scolded back.

I closed the door and let him yowl until Mom couldn't stand it anymore and let him back in.

My sister threw OatieBits at nothing in particular.

"Bad Boy," she said to no one.

The next day, my brother decided to come with me to school. Owen the cat stared at his empty bowl, protesting loudly.

"Oh, WHAT?" Mom said. "I just fed you!" Both the food and water bowl looked as though they were licked clean. "Hush now. You are just fine."

"Meow," Owen said with a wounded expression.

"Bad Boy," my sister said, looking out the window.

My brother wasn't at breakfast. "Mom's not ready," he had said. He waited for me outside. When I met him on the front sidewalk, he was eating something crunchy, but he turned away so I wouldn't see. He didn't look so good—kind of pale, and thin in the cheeks. I hoped he wasn't getting sick.

"Just a minute," I said, and I ran to the other side of the cul-de-sac to knock on Jamal's door. He had been sick since Sunday, and I wanted to show him my new brother. He'd never have believed it otherwise.

Jamal's mother answered the door with a two-year-old on one hip and a five-year-old attached to one leg. She wore stockings and heels and a jacket that looked like a suit but it's for ladies. She works for the governor. She also sends a lot of emails, like my dad. I wondered if her laptop also caught on fire.

"I'm sorry, honey," she said. "Jamal is still sick. And the nanny is late. And all kinds of heck is breaking loose around here. You haven't seen our nanny, have you? She was supposed to be here an hour ago."

I hadn't, so I waved good-bye and went to find my brother. He was standing next to a backpack and a bicycle lying on the ground. The backpack had a patch on it from a band that I've never heard, but that Jamal's nanny has said again and again is the best ever, but she can't play them for us because they use too many swears.

"Don't those belong to the nanny?" I asked.

My brother burped. "I don't think so," he said.

"Whose stuff is this?"

"It all belonged to someone. But now I think it belongs to the ground."

Like I said, my brother was new around here. There was a lot he didn't understand. And so we went to school.

I tried to tell my teacher about my brother, but I could barely see her over the stack of papers on her desk. She used a rubber stamp to grade each paper. "Try a little harder," the stamp said. She stamped each paper the exact same way.

The seat next to mine was Jamal's, but since he wasn't there, I told my brother to sit there instead. Right away, he wiggled and fidgeted in his seat.

"I don't think I like school," he said.

"No one likes school," I said. "But we all still have to go."

My brother started doodling on Jamal's stuff. He ripped out a piece of notebook paper, wrote something down, folded it up in the shape of a star, and passed it to me. "I wish I was home," the note said. I rolled my eyes. I folded the note back up in its star shape, and put it in my pocket.

"Yeah, me too. We'll get back before you know it."

My brother was kind of whiny, I started to realize. And I was annoyed. But if there's one thing I learned from Jamal, brothers—even, apparently, the ones that show up after a wish—are kind of annoying.

"I'm hungry," my brother said. There were dark circles under his eyes. His skin was as pale as bone.

"Well," I said. "You should have come down to breakfast. You need to eat, you know."

"I did," he complained.

"Really? What did you eat?"

My brother burped again—a loud, juicy one. An earring popped out of his mouth. "Um, nothing," my brother said.

"Okay, students," my teacher said. "Everybody up and check your job chart. Tasks are to be completed in ten minutes."

We all got up and checked the job chart. It changed every day. Today, I was in charge of arranging the markers by color. Other kids had to take out the recycling or the trash, or take the lunch orders to the main office. I saw that Jamal was in charge of feeding Humphrey, our class hamster. I was about to tell my brother to do it, but I didn't see him anywhere. *So slippery, that guy!* I thought. I organized the markers and sat down. My brother sat down next to me with a large bulge in one cheek. It wriggled a bit.

"Hey," I said. "What's that in your—" But I couldn't finish.

"Children?" my teacher gasped. "Oh my goodness, children! Where is Humphrey?"

My brother gulped. Then, he started to whistle.

That's when I started getting suspicious.

We searched every nook and cranny, but it was no use. Humphrey was gone.

My brother rubbed his belly.

That's it, I thought.

My brother and I didn't talk very much on the way home.

"Why are you walking so fast?" my brother said. He was walking funny—a sort of shuffly, stumbly lope. And his eyes were starting to smudge, as though they were slicked with ink instead of tears. Every time he blinked, they were a little bit darker. He licked his lips. Even his tongue looked weird. Also, he was starting to stink—like old eggs.

"Walkin' normal," I said, even though I wasn't. I wasn't at all. I was hurrying. My brother stumbled. He started falling farther and farther behind. I didn't care.

"I'm hungry," he whined. I walked even faster. I glanced back and saw my brother hungrily eyeing a squirrel in a tree. I turned the corner and ran straight to Jamal's house.

His grandma answered the door. I was surprised to see her.

"Where's the nanny?" I asked.

Mrs. Watkins shrugged. "Never showed up," she said. She patted my cheek. "Oh, don't look so worried! I'm sure it was just a mix-up."

But I was sure it wasn't. I handed her an envelope. The outside said, "For Jamal's eyes only." I had underlined the word "only" ten times so his brothers would know it wasn't for them.

"Is he feeling better?" I asked. "Jamal, I mean."

"He's on the mend. He was bouncing off the walls just a little bit ago, wanting to check on you. He went on and on about something following you out of the scrub lot, but I'm sure that was just the fever. Because you boys know better than to go under that fence." She let that sit for a minute while she gave me a hard look.

"Umm," I said. "Right. Could you give him this note please?"

She said she would and I took off, running like a demon to the corner and waiting there like it was no big deal. I watched my brother as he came up over the rise. He smiled when he saw me. I guess he wasn't hungry anymore. His teeth flashed in the afternoon light. They were thin and pointy and sharp as knives.

Owen waited for us at the screen door. He arched his

back and showed his teeth. He pressed his ears flat against the top of his skull. My brother licked his lips.

"Nice kitty," he said. "Sweet kitty."

Owen screeched.

"I don't think you should go through the front door," I said. "Climb through the window instead."

"Are you sure? I'm feeling ready to be part of the family. Or to have the family be part of me. It means the same thing, you know."

"It doesn't mean the same thing at all," I said. "Just climb through the window and stop arguing."

"You said you wanted me. You wrote it down and everything."

"I did," I soothed. "I mean I do. I just don't think Mom is ready to meet you." I paused. "Yet," I added hastily.

"Mom is sweet," he said, and his eyes got even darker.

"Off you go," I said.

I watched him climb the trellis into my room.

"WE DON'T EAT MOMS!" I called to him as he reached my window.

"We'll see," my brother called back.

I went into the kitchen and grabbed everything I could think of. Cold cuts. Cheese. A Tupperware of yesterday's stew.

"Boy," my sister said, throwing a handful of OatieBits at me. I grabbed the box.

My brother was waiting for me on my bed. His color looked a little better, and his eyes, while dark, had a bright sheen to them. He must have just eaten, I figured. I glanced around the room and saw that all of my fish and one of my guinea pigs were nowhere to be seen. I frowned.

"I don't think I want a brother anymore," I said.

"Everyone says that," my brother said. "But secretly they love their brothers very much. This is common knowledge."

"But I mean it."

"Well. It's too late. A wish is a wish." And then he smiled. The razor edges of his teeth flashed. I shivered.

Owen hissed at the other side of the door.

It was right then when I realized that I really loved that cat. And that I always had.

That night, after we brushed our teeth, my brother made a big show about getting into my bed and pulling the covers up to his chin with a sigh.

"That's not where you sleep," I said. I did not say, *You sleep under the bed with the monsters* out loud, but I thought it.

"My bed now," he said. "It's your turn to take the floor. He closed his eyes. "Hmmmmm. Am I hungry or tired?

That is the question. I can't seem to be able to decide."

"Fine," I said. "I'll take the floor. Just go to sleep, will you?"

When Mom came in to kiss me good night, she kissed my brother instead. She didn't notice his sharp teeth or his bone-pale skin or his inky eyes. "Good night, my little zookeeper," she said, kissing my brother's forehead.

"Oh, Mom," he said. "You are just so sweet."

I kicked the mattress. No one noticed.

"I'm here too, Mom," I said. She didn't say anything. I don't think she heard me.

"Mom," my brother said. "I'm scared there's something under the bed. Will you check for me?" He was trying, and failing, to keep from laughing. Like this was the funniest thing in the world.

"You're too old for that, honey," Mom said.

"Do it anyway," he insisted with a snicker.

"Fine." She knelt down, knees cracking, and laid her hands on the ground. She rested her head on the floor. She looked right at me. I smiled. She stared right past my face to the shadowed wall.

"I don't see anything, honey," she said, her eyes losing their focus.

I felt my skin go cold.

"Nothing at all?" my brother said with a giggle.

"Nothing at all," Mom said with a yawn.

"Well. I guess we should be careful what we wish for," my brother said.

But he wasn't saying that to Mom. He was talking to me.

I didn't think I'd fall asleep after that, but I guess I must have. Later that night I had a dream about the unbuildable land. I don't think my mom and dad ever knew about the well. They certainly never mentioned it. But in my dream, there they both were, standing at the edge of the well, peering down into the darkness.

"Whoever dug a well that deep sure didn't want anything coming back up," my mom said.

"There's a reason why you're not allowed back here, Arne," Dad said. "When will you *listen?*"

I woke up to the sound of my sister.

"Bad Boy," she said. "Bad Boy."

I scrambled out from under the bed. It was the middle of the night, and the house was quiet except for my sister's voice. My brother stood in the hallway. His face was so pale and gaunt, it looked more like a skull than a face. His eyes were still black, but his pupils took on a bit of a reddish glow. In his hands was the soup pot. In the soup pot was my sister. "Boy," she said, pointing to me. "Bad Boy," she said, pointing to my brother.

"We don't eat babies," I said firmly. I lifted my sister out of the pot and directed my brother downstairs. "*Especially* not sisters."

"But I'm *so hungry*," he complained. I gave him the bag of cat food. I don't know how much was in there, but it had to be at least ten pounds. He ate it greedily. All of it. I held my sister on my hip, both arms tight around her body. She stared at my brother and wrinkled her nose.

"Bad Boy," she said. "Yuck."

It wasn't going to hold off his hunger forever, I knew that. But I figured it would satisfy him at least until the next morning. Which was all I needed. Because I had a plan.

I slept on the floor of my sister's room for the rest of that night. Owen guarded the door to my mom's room. I realized with a start that one of my rabbits was missing. I hadn't noticed it before. Some zookeeper I am.

I wondered about my rats. I hoped they made it out okay.

Before the sun came up, I went to the window to see if Jamal's reading light was on. It was. He usually woke up early to read because he is an overachiever—something that I used to make fun of him about, but vowed to never do again. I tapped the window a few times, and flickered the light next to the window to get his attention.

Remember what I told you before about Morse Code? Seriously, everyone should learn it.

I left the light on and grabbed the handle on the shade, pulling it down and letting it up, over and over in long and short pulses. I waited, hoping he had seen the whole message.

Jamal waited for a minute. Then he sent two messages back.

The first one was: "I told you so."

The second one was: "I'll be waiting for you in front of the house at seven."

I brought my sister downstairs and put her in her high chair. My dad was already sitting at the table, his hands tapping the placemat as if it might suddenly turn into a new laptop.

"Look who's so helpful," he said, picking up his newspaper and starting to read.

"Good Boy," my sister said. I rubbed her head. She wasn't so bad, really, as babies go.

My brother came into the kitchen. He sat next to my dad. My dad didn't seem to notice there were two boys in the room. He kept reading his newspaper like everything was normal. My sister kept trying to explain it to him.

"Bad Boy," my sister said, pointing at my brother. She threw OatieBits at him. My dad still didn't get it. Maybe this thing with my brother was like the trail in the unbuildable land—you can only really notice the situation if you know where to look.

"How did you sleep, Arne?" my dad said to his newspaper.

"Not so good, Pop," my brother said. I realized that his fingernails had grown. They curved out of his fingertips like talons.

"Hmmm," Dad said, turning the page. "Maybe you should eat something."

My brother shot a look at my sister.

"Bad Boy," my sister said again.

"That's not fair, sweetie," my dad said, turning the page. "Your brother is a very good boy."

I handed my brother the entire plate of English muffins.

"Depends on how you look at it, Dad," I said. He still didn't notice that there were two of us. He turned the page again. "Sometimes I'm good and sometimes I'm bad. Like everyone, I suppose."

"Boy," my sister said to me. "Bad Boy," she said to my

brother. She had no trouble telling us apart.

My brother gave a long, hungry look at my sister before letting his face fall heavily on the plate, swallowing English muffin after English muffin without even chewing them first.

"Don't be a piggy, Arne," my dad said, turning the page.

"Sorry, Dad," my brother and I said in unison.

"I'm still hungry," my brother whispered.

"Come on," I said. "I know how to fix that."

I said good-bye to my dad and my sister while my brother ate an entire dozen eggs—raw, shells and all, throwing each one up and catching it in his mouth with a crunch and a swallow. My mom told me to take out the trash and told my brother to make sure to bring home the Picture Day forms. She didn't notice we were separate people either.

Jamal waited for us on his front steps.

He looked at me.

He looked at my brother. He shook his head slowly.

"I'm hungry," my brother said, staring at Jamal.

Jamal rolled his eyes. "Oh, for crying out loud," he said. He glared at me. "Didn't I tell you about brothers? Well? Didn't I?"

"I know," I said.

"Has he been wrecking stuff?" Jamal asked. He gave my brother a hard look. "Brothers are *always* wrecking stuff. It's what they *do*."

"You don't know the half of it," I said.

"Are you sweet?" my brother asked.

"No," Jamal said, showing his teeth. "I'm poisonous. Ask my brothers."

My brother slumped a bit. "Oh," he said. "Darn."

"Come on," I said, slipping my arms into my backpack straps. "Let's go to the picnic spot." I gave Jamal a sharp look. "You know which one I'm talking about, right?"

"We're going to eat?" my brother said, brightening up.

"Yup. Lots of stuff." I took his hand and pulled him along. "We're gonna have a feast."

"Meow," Owen the cat said, following a safe distance behind.

We ran to the edge of the subdivision and crawled under the fence. The sky turned dark, and huge gray clouds swirled over the tops of the cottonwood trees, making them creak and moan. The trail was hard to see, even when we were looking for it. And the air smelled gross. Like old eggs.

"What's that smell?" Jamal said, wrinkling his nose.

"I know that smell," my brother said, and he had a wistful look on his face.

"Of course you do," I said. "Home sweet home."

"Sweet," my brother said, and he closed his eyes.

This is going to sound strange to you—heck, it sounds strange to me, and I was *there*—but I knew right then that I was going to miss my brother. Despite everything. Because he was my *brother*, you know?

And I couldn't undo my wish—I knew I couldn't. But what if my brother made a wish? What if I tricked him into making one?

There were rocks in my bag. Three of them. With notes. And there was rope in my bag, too. I just hoped my plan would work.

It had to work.

I really didn't want my baby sister to turn into anyone's breakfast, least of all my brother's. And I was the only one who could stop it.

We got to the edge of the well and sat down. I opened my bag and pulled out a sandwich for my brother. He ate it without swallowing. I tossed him another, and another and another. Each one, he snatched from the air, like he was a trained dolphin. *Snap, snap, snap,* went his jaws. He swallowed each one with a choke and a gulp. And each time his jaws opened wider and wider and wider, like a rusty hinge working out the kinks.

"Is your brother part snake?" Jamal whispered.

"He's part *something,* that's for sure," I whispered back.

I reached into the bag, grabbing another sandwich with one hand and a bundle of rope with the other. I tossed my brother the sandwich. "Still hungry?" I said. "Well, okay." I handed the rope to Jamal. "Slippery Eight. Quick."

The night before, in my sister's room, I had written wishes on pieces of paper, and tied them onto some rocks. I had color-coded them so I wouldn't get confused.

The wind picked up and it started to rain. Lightning cracked the sky. Jamal looked up, his face clouded with worry.

"We should get inside," he said.

"Lightning can't hurt me," my brother said.

"Meow," said Owen. He hissed at my brother. My brother showed Owen his teeth, which shut him up pretty quick. Owen scampered up the nearest cottonwood tree and perched on a low branch, keeping his eyes on my brother.

I decided to try my first wish. The one on red paper. It said, "I wish I never had a brother."

Without telling anyone I was about to do it, I threw

the rock into the well. The sky flashed. The well belched up a cloud of gross-smelling mist. Then it belched up a spout of dark water. Which was also gross-smelling. Then it belched out a rock. My rock.

"Uh-oh," Jamal said, holding his rope tied in a perfect Slippery Eight. He didn't even have to look. He is that good.

My brother glared at me. His eyes were bright red. His face was bone. His teeth weren't just sharp and pointy. They were fangs. Each tooth was a fang. Each finger was a claw. He uncurled from the ground. He raised his fists to the sky and howled. Owen howled. I think I howled too.

"You just wished you didn't have a brother!" my brother said. "I can't *believe* you! I would *never* do that to you!"

"I know," I said. "I'm sorry."

But I wasn't sorry at all. I grabbed the second rock. The one with the blue paper. I threw it into the well. Again, lightning flashed and the well belched—first mist, then water, then the rock. My brother started slapping his ears and stomping on the ground. (Had his feet always been claws? They couldn't have been. Still, I was getting a clearer picture as to what my brother actually *was*. Maybe *he* was like the path in the unbuildable land, too. Maybe you could only see the true parts of him if you knew where to look.)

"You wished that I'd go back to where I came from? MEAN!" My brother started to cry. "Well, joke's on you. You can't undo your own wishes, *dummy*." He walked over and grabbed the last rock. There was a piece of notebook paper tied to it. The notebook paper was folded in the shape of a star. "You don't get to throw in your wish, *and* I'm going to eat your friend. How do you like *that*, dummy?"

"Well," I said. "I think that's a terrible idea. Jamal! The rope!"

Quick as lightning, Jamal threw the rope around my brother, cinching it tight. My brother clenched his razor-sharp claws around the rock. There was no way we were going to get it out of his hand.

Jamal wrapped the rope around and around my brother, dodging his teeth.

"Quick, Arne!" Jamal shouted. "Push him in!"

But I couldn't. He was my brother. I couldn't push him into the well.

My brother laughed—a high, wicked, demonish laugh. "Doesn't matter *what* you try to do. You can't undo your own wish. Even if you push me in, I'll still come back. And when I do, I'll eat the baby. And then I'll eat the mom, and then the dad, and then your stupid friend and his family too. And everyone else in the neighborhood. And your teacher. I don't think I'll ever be full."

"But not me," I said.

"Of course not you. You're my brother. You're the only home I have. I used to have a home. But I don't anymore." And he sounded almost sad. In fact, I think he really *was* sad. I had taken him away from his home with my stupid wish. That had to hurt, right?

And I was about to explain it, I really was. And maybe if I had, he would have done it on his own. In the end, it didn't matter. Owen the cat, with a loud warrior yawp, leaped from the low branch of the cottonwood tree. In midair, he grabbed the end of the rope and leaped across the well, pulling my brother behind. My brother, losing his balance, toppled over and fell into the well.

"You!" he screamed as he disappeared into the darkness. "*You meanies!*"

And then I heard the rock fall out of his hands and hit the side of the well. And then I didn't hear anything. Just the wind in the sumac bushes and the rustle of the cottonwood trees.

The old well had nothing to say. Nothing at all.

"Meow," Owen said from the other side of the well. He

sat down and began licking his left paw.

"I agree," I said, slumping down and falling heavily onto the ground.

"But—" Jamal got up and looked into the darkness of the well. There was no belch. There was no sound. There was just the foul-smelling wind and the dark. Jamal squinted, trying to see as far as he could. "Won't he come back? He said he'd come back."

"It wasn't my wish," I said. "It was his. He wrote a note to me in class that he wished he could go home. I thought before that he meant our home—that is, my home. But now I'm not so sure."

And I'm still not.

"In any case," I continued, "it was his wish, and he was holding the rock, and he let the rock go into the well. So it looks like the wish stuck."

And so far, it has. And I don't know for sure if my brother is happy about it.

All I know is this: When we walked back through the unbuildable land, the air turned sweet and the sky cleared up, and the lightning went away. And what's more, there was a funny sound coming from the rustling branches of the sumac bushes and the cottonwood trees. "Thank you," they seemed to whisper. "Thank you." I know that sounds crazy. But I swear it's the truth.

When we got back, both Jamal and I faced Certain Grounding on account of the fact that we had skipped school. My mom and his grandma both waited for us in our respective front yards, their arms folded tightly across their chests.

"Do you have *any* idea how worried we've been?" my mom shouted.

"Are you aware, young man, that your mother and father are both on the phone with the police this very minute?" Jamal's grandma roared.

Both my mom and Jamal's grandma grabbed us by our respective ears and hauled us inside. In spite of that, Jamal and I glanced at each other and winked. We had both practiced what our excuses would be—collecting soil and water samples to analyze for our Concerned Environmentalist badges in scouts. It is too bad that there isn't a Returning Demons to their Bottomless Pit badge, because we totally would have earned it.

"Look who decided to come back," my dad said. I thought he was talking about me, but he wasn't. My dad sat on the bench in the kitchen. Jeeves and Bertie, my two rats, sat perched on each of his knees. They inclined their noses toward me and sniffed, as though making sure I really was who I appeared to be.

"Hi, guys," I said, gathering my rats in my arms. I was so glad to see them, I thought I might cry.

"I told you they'd come back," my mom said.

"Must mean the house is now free of ghosts," my dad said. "Silly rats. Don't they know ghosts and goblins can't actually hurt you?"

I figured I'd just let my dad believe that. I didn't want to destroy his innocence.

My dad, as it turned out, decided to take the day off. After first chewing me out for skipping class without permission, he told me that my bad behavior made him realize that he needed to cut some hours out of the work week.

"Starting today, I'll be volunteering in your classroom," my dad said. "So I can see firsthand what goes on in that school of yours. And then, young man, you and I are playing Monopoly." He had already taken out the box.

"Boy," my sister said, picking up an OatieBit and throwing it, in one clean, long arc, right at my face. I opened my mouth wide and caught it.

"Good Arne," the baby said.

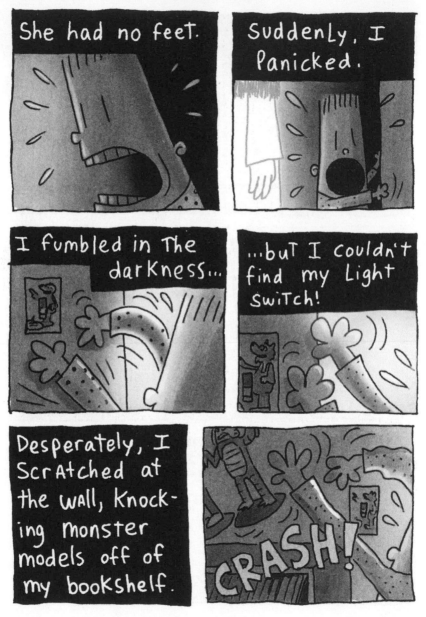

135

137

138

MARCOS AT THE RIVER
BY DANIEL JOSÉ OLDER

I haven't been back here since that night two years ago when my father died. Then, it was summer. I wore a red T-shirt and even though it was late, the sky still glowed purple and red over the abandoned sugar factory across the river. Now it's October, and the night is everywhere, pushing through the skyscraper corridors on the howling wind. The air tightens and releases like giant gasps; the whole city seems like it's trembling, waiting for the storm to hit.

That night two years ago, my abuela sent me to get my dad—he'd gone for another of his walks down by the East River. I was alone, but I felt strong, excited by her trust in me and full of the joy of the city around me, right up until the gunshot shattered all that. Today, a dozen shimmering spirits hover in the air behind me. They stir slightly; I hear them rustling and their guttural moans and impossible whispers. We look out at the river, and then the sky opens up and it begins to rain.

After it happened, everybody had questions, but I could tell they didn't really want to know. The cops, for instance. They sat me down in an ugly gray room with bad words and love poems scratched into the ugly gray walls. They gave me soda and some old candy, and one sat down and leaned in real close, way too close, and said, "Marcos, I understand you haven't been speaking. Well, I want to tell you something. It's very important that you speak and tell us what happened that night, okay, little buddy?"

Like I had *chosen* to stop speaking.

Like I didn't *want* to speak.

Back then, I was still trying. That was before I realized that me trying made people think I actually would and then they'd get frustrated when I didn't—because I didn't, hard as I tried. I never ever spoke, still haven't spoken— and then frustration turned to rage and rage to apologies, apologies to discomfort and then absence.

Now I don't even try.

But that was before all that, so when the cop asked me

to tell him what happened, I opened my mouth like I'd been doing and nothing came out, not even a little gulpy noise. A therapist came in, asked the same questions, gave me some paper and markers to draw with, looked at me with big, blue, sorrowful eyes like I might somehow feel bad for her and start talking so she wouldn't shatter.

Didn't work.

Nothing works.

My abuela sees the spirits too, although she probably doesn't see much else through all those cataracts. She wears gigantic librarian glasses that make her eyes look like foggy planets, too big for her wrinkly face. But she's been seeing the spirits even longer than I have. Says they been around her since she was little like me, but never this many, and never this wet.

More important, she understands them. Back when those glowing shadows first started showing up, Abuela was the one who taught me not to be afraid. I was anyway, at first. I mean, of course I was! The night by the river was still all I could see, all I could think about, that thick, wet air all I could smell—and then I walked outside our housing project. It was the evening of my father's funeral—no body; they never found him—and I had a suit on, all tight and itchy. There, shimmering over the walking path to our building, was a spirit. I knew what it was—Abuela had told me stories. I could make out its human form beneath that shroud, just looked like skin and bones, but I knew I wasn't just making it up: The pavement all around it was soaked. Water dripped from its barely-there arms, its grinning jaw.

I turned and ran. What would you do?

The truth is, if I open my mouth, I won't be able to stop what comes out. See, it's all there, the whole night, lurking, waiting. Festering. Has been for two years. I get flashes of it: My father yells, sees me, his eyes frantic, then looks at someone else. A heavy splash. A shadow, running. That's it. I know the rest is there, but I can't look at it. It's like the sun. I'm sure I'll go blind. And that's blocking everything else. There's a two-year-long traffic jam of words in the back of my throat, but it's gridlocked: a standstill. I accept it now, and mostly the social workers and therapists do too. Abuela keeps talking to me like one day I'll answer, and I don't mind.

Earlier tonight, as NY1 blared about the approaching storm, Abuela stirred a pot of frijoles negros and sighed. "You have to do something," she said. I looked up from the TV. Thick garlicky steam heavied up the air, and the sound of bubbling beans mixed with stern warnings about evacuation procedures and flood levels.

Me? my wide eyes said. She didn't even bother looking at me.

The house was full of spirits. We're used to it at this point. After the one outside, more came. They'd leave again, or just hang there, dripping and gargling and be gone when I'd come back. But then they started gathering in Abuela's apartment, gradually at first. I went away to a care center and they were there too, and then I came back and more had shown up. "We can't live like this," Abuela said. "These spirits . . . they are not happy. They are not home."

I muted the TV and padded past two hovering spirits into the kitchen. I didn't want to be a burden to my abuela—she was all I had left, all that was keeping me from going back to one of those creepy care centers. A thin puddle covered the tiled floor, no matter how much we mopped. I stepped gingerly through it and stood beside my abuela as she opened the oven to check on the chicken. "Whatever it is you must do, do it, Marcos. Soon. I wish I could tell you, but they won't speak to me."

She handed me the mop and I shoved a layer of river water off the kitchen floor, swatting spirits out of the way.

Outside, trees danced and whispered in the wind and, farther away, ambulance sirens wailed.

"Manhattan is on high floodwater alert as the storm front approaches from south of the city," the news anchor said, waking me. "The East River is poised to breach into the Lower East Side at any moment." I felt the truth of it in my gut. The river is coming to us. I couldn't ignore it anymore, couldn't look away. The river is coming to us. "The mayor's office has told New York One that if anyone hasn't yet evacuated from the designated zones, they are urged to seek high ground and shelter."

Abuela was knocked out in her easy chair, her belly rising and falling in the flickering light of the TV. The spirits flitted and fluttered around the apartment—seemed like there were even more of them now . . . eight, nine, ten! The kitchen floor shone with a newly formed puddle. The leather couch rustled as I climbed off it, but otherwise the only sounds were the whistle of the wind and water dripdropping from the glowing shrouds around me. Abuela slept on as I tiptoed to the door, pulled on my rubber boots and rain jacket, and then slipped out of the apartment.

Spirits. They lined the hallways of my building, at least a dozen on my floor, and I could see more shimmering from the stairwell. They followed me in a quiet, dripping procession, lighting my way down the steps to the lobby and out into the storm. The streets were empty of people but full of movement: Trees thrashed and plastic bags whipped through the gray air. Way off at the far side of the housing project, someone ran for a taxi that sped off without stopping. I turned toward the river and began to walk.

Halfway across the pedestrian bridge over the highway, I paused. A few cars passed underneath, windshield wipers keeping furious time, headlights glaring through the gathering gray. Behind me, the crowd of spirits thinned to a line almost three blocks long so they could cross the bridge in single file. I raised my hands as if to demand an answer, but the spirits had nothing to say—they just hung there, glowing, dripping, waiting. A stream of water ran the length of the bridge and spilled down the ramp up ahead. Beyond that, a few trees swished in the little park along the crashing river.

Now it's raining, pouring actually, and black waves crash up onto the walkway. A hundred spirits stand behind me, dripping and waiting. He's out there, somewhere, my dad. I used to check each spirit, once I stopped being so freaked out by them, for some sign that it was him: a familiar look in those ghostly eyes maybe, or a scrap of the blue T-shirt he was wearing that night. But no, none of these spirits are him. My dad is out there, his broken body slowly corroding in the dark waters. If he has a spirit, it's probably waiting for . . .

Waiting for what?

I turn to the shrouds behind me, a tiny city of them now, their haunted glow lighting up the night. Waiting for what? They seem to nod collectively, goading me forward. *Waiting for me?* I eye the wild waves as they spill onto the walkway around me, ankle-deep, and then recede. The spirits started leaving the river after my father died in it. One by one, then many at a time, and now . . . hundreds. And the water itself is trying to escape. Escape a spirit that won't rest.

Waiting for what?

And then I know. *Whatever it is you must do, do it, Marcos,* Abuela had said. *Soon.* The one thing I haven't done, couldn't do, all this time.

I close my eyes.

The first word that comes out is more like a grunt: "Egh." I cough and try again, feel the collective strength of the spirits behind me rustle and gather.

"It."

I spit the word out and then say it louder to match the howling wind.

"It was warm."

A full sentence.

"A warm night."

Out in the river, something breaches the surface of the water. Something bright.

"I wore a red T-shirt!" I yell, and the light gets brighter. "And the sky still glowed purple and red over the abandoned sugar factory across the river."

I can see its form now, a glowing body suspended in midair, arms flailing to either side.

"Abuela sent me to come get you, because dinner was ready." The wind picks up and I have to yell louder to keep from being drowned out by the crashing waves. "And when I got here, there was someone else here . . . a man. I didn't see his face." The glowing man hovers toward me, hands outstretched. "You had your blue T-shirt on and you were . . . you were arguing, I think. I heard you tell him something, but I didn't know what. So I hid in this bush." The rain splatters against my face; I'm soaked all the way to the bone, but I barely feel it. Another wave crashes around me and I yell louder. "I hid but you saw me, Dad. You looked at me and then back and then yelled something and then I heard the bang and the bang was the whole world and you fell backward, into the river with a heavy splash, and I didn't see the man's face or know who he was, but I was scared and he started turning, so I ran and ran and ran."

I'm crying. My tears mix with the rainwater, the river water, the spirit water, and it feels good to say it, even though it hurts. When I wipe my eyes, the shining spirit is right in front of me, and I see my dad's face for one full second—he's smiling—and then he's gone. All the lights that made him up scatter out into the sky and disappear. The rain is still falling, but the wind has settled. The water retreats and one by one, the river spirits shuffle past me, each one pausing to nod with respect before it vanishes into the dark waters.

"You went out?" Abuela almost jumps out of her easy chair when I come in. "In this weather?" Then she looks around; the sudden emptiness of the apartment dawns on her. "They're gone." The warm smell of arroz con pollo lingers. She sees me dripping wet, my tear- and rain-soaked face.

"I did it," I say. My first words to another person in two years. Well, a living person anyway. "I told the story of what happened . . ." And before I can say "that night,"

Abuela has crossed the apartment in two bounds and wrapped around me.

"Ay, m'ijo," she coos, stroking my back.

"But I didn't solve the murder, I don't know what happened. I just . . . I just said what I saw. And the spirits went back to the river and the flooding stopped."

"Sometimes, you just have to tell the story," Abuela says. "And that can change the world. What matters is that you found your voice, Marcos."

"It was by the river all along," I say, hugging her back. "Right where I left it."

COCONUT HEADS
BY RITA WILLIAMS-GARCIA

This is how I know something's different about my mother. My waste not, want not, save-don't-spend mother says to me, while we're all next to the JetBlue check-in line, "It's not too late. I can still get you a ticket." She takes a blue booklet from her purse and sings, "I have your passport!"

My father pretends he doesn't notice a switch's been made, but I know she's not my real mom. Real Mom would say, "Buy a last-minute ticket at these prices? Do you think I'm made of money?" Instead, this changeling mom repeats herself and waits for a change of heart. She smiles and begs at the same time, wanting me to board the plane with her. But I don't care how much she smiles. I'm not getting on a plane to Jamaica with her. Being stuck up in the hills with the "changeling," treacherous cousins, and goats isn't my idea of a vacation.

"I'll stay with Dad," I tell her. I try to be nice. Respectful. Act like it's no big deal.

Still, she gives me big, sad eyes and her face morphs into her crying face. "But how could you not come with me? Colin would have had his bags packed at least a week in advance. He couldn't wait to go back home."

"There's still time to call him," I say, and I know I'm being cruel, but I'm not going. "I'm sure he'll drop everything to fly to Jamaica."

"Don't be silly, Winston. He's locked into his studies."

Not likely. My brother just doesn't want to come home and face Mom. I eavesdrop. I know. One minute she's proud of him, the next minute she's yelling at him. Colin's not studying. He's hiding. What kind of college guy takes summer classes when he makes dean's list? My brother knows something's up with Mom and would rather stay 750 miles away in his dorm room.

"Please, darling." She's all sweetness. So sweet I inch closer to Dad. That doesn't stop her. "Please, please."

No matter what she says, I turn my head east, then west, and in no time her begging smile flatlines.

Here it comes: the flip.

She stamps both feet. "I can't believe this. My own son would rather stay here doing scritch-scratch"—she means my comic book drawings—"than spend a lovely vacation with his dear mother and his family, and soak up his roots." I want to say "half roots," but now is not the time to remind her that Dad's from the South, because there's more foot stamping. "I can't believe it!" she wails. "I can-*not* believe what my ears are hearing." She looks less like a medical doctor entrusted with human lives, and more like a two-year-old.

Who is this woman and where is Dr. Bailey, a.k.a. my mom? I turn away like I don't know her.

Dad speaks up. "If Winston doesn't want to fly to Jamaica, he'll stay home." He's extra gentle, probably hoping she won't go bananas like she did at the frozen yogurt place last night. All I can do on the airport ID check line is stare off like it's not happening. Dad says, "Go home, dear. See the folks. Send our love." He pretends he doesn't see her eyes narrow at him, or the beads of sweat dotting her forehead, neck, and nose. He fans her with his hand, but she slaps it away so hard the whole line must hear the slap, though no one looks at us.

"Stop it!" she hisses.

Dad tilts his head toward her and speaks slowly and

firmly. "Calm down, Claudia. Calm it down."

This only makes things worse. The sweat beads now stream until her face is red and glossy. "Calm nothing! My own son won't come home with me!" People on line interrupt their travel chatter and turn toward the commotion. I'm aware of the TSA agents in dark uniforms studying us. My mother's fevered glare dares anyone to say anything to her, and my father keeps his eye on her just in case. I don't want us to be tonight's airline news story or for my mad mom to go viral on the internet. I just want her ID checked, her shoes thrown in a plastic bin, while we wave at her from a distance as she and her carry-on go through the scanners. It's not happening fast enough.

"I don't see why he won't come with me," she steams.

"Winston has plenty to do here," Dad says, back to his calm self. "I'll keep him busy."

We all know this is a lie. Dad just basically leaves me alone, which is fine. I'm not five.

"Don't let him eat pizza all day long." She brings it down a notch, but it's too late. The TSA agents stare us down as we near the head of the line.

"I won't, dear."

Dad rolls her carry-on bag and we follow. I stay a little closer to Dad. Now only three people stand ahead of her at the line for ticket and ID inspection, and it looks like they're all together, so technically, we're next. Mom sweetens and she and Dad stick out their necks and lips to bird-peck each other. Then she wraps me in a hug, her arms super cold, then kisses my forehead and the top of my bald head, which isn't really bald, but is close enough that that's what my dread-headed cousins call it. Bald-headed. Baldie bean. Her lips are kind of warm, almost hot on my head, and I rub the hot, sticky Mom spit away.

"Winston!" She flips from sweetness to shrieking. But she's up next and I say, "Bye, Mom," and I'm sort of glad she's showing the agent her passport.

In the car, Dad says, "It's hard on her. She looks forward to sharing this trip with you and your brother."

I shake my head no. "She looks forward to sharing this trip with Colin."

Colin is the one she really wants with her so they can get deep with the patois and talk cricket matches. Colin was raised in Jamaica and lived with the cousins and Grandma, Grandpa, and uncles and aunts until he was six. Mom and Dad were med students in the States and couldn't study and take care of a baby, so they brought him to Jamaica to live up in the hills with my grandparents in Brown's Town while they finished school and residencies. By the time they sent for Colin, I was on the way. My mother loves how Colin is like his cousins, Jamaican through and through. She even calls him her countryman. I'm a different story. Except for the food Mom cooks, and understanding patois when I hear her talking to relatives, I grew up a "Yankee bwai," like Dad—even though, technically, Dad is Southern.

I call Jamaica "Jamaica," but Colin calls it home. My first summer in Jamaica, my father had to take off from the hospital, fly to Jamaica, and bring me home. After that, my trips "home" didn't last longer than one week of being called "baldie bean" and running from the goats. It was one thing to have no choice and have to be dragged to Jamaica. It's another when you're old enough to make your own toast, get around town, and have a choice. You choose no goats and no cousins.

I've already blown summer day camp, so Dad drops me off at the library, where I meet up with Robbie Laszlo, my neighbor and collaborator. We meet in the teen room or at my house because I'm no longer welcome at Robbie's. It doesn't matter how many times you say, "It was an accident," and clearly it was, but Mrs. Laszlo couldn't stand to look at me, which is unfair. She knows what her grandmother went through to smuggle that lamp out of Budapest. Why keep an irreplaceable treasure in plain sight, where anything could happen to it? It doesn't matter what I say or do. A thousand "sorry"s can't fix it.

We take up a whole table with our tablets and sketch pads and get cranking on *Pyra*, our weekly comic strip. We post it for subscribers only, but neither Robbie nor I code well enough, so our site's totally hackable. For now we just post it and hope for subscribers.

This week Pyra meets her archnemesis, Ice-X, who threatens to extinguish Pyra's eternal flame. I draw Ice-X and all other guest villains while Robbie sketches and colors Pyra, who's really naked until he covers her in flames. We haven't figured out if Pyra's good or evil. Just that she throws flames if you piss her off.

"Win," he says, "you're stupid." I don't bother to look up. "I wish she took me."

"That's the problem right there," I say. He shrugs like he doesn't know what I mean, but he does. "How many times have you been to Jamaica?"

He answers, "Four. But one doesn't count because I was a baby."

"Okay, throw that one out. You flew to Jamaica three times."

He shrugs again. Each time he went, he'd rush back to show me his tan before it faded.

"And when did you go?" I asked. "What part of the year?"

More shrugging. "Winter. Holidays."

"Where'd you stay?" This is all setup to make my point. I know where the Laszlos stayed.

We say it in unison. "Sun Splash."

"Home of the best manmade waterfall," I add, because Robbie never lets me forget it.

He waits for me to wrap it up. "Yeah. And?"

"If my mom said, we're escaping the mosquitoes, goats, and the cook-a-brain heat of the hills, and staying at the Sun Splash resort—chlorinated pool, manmade waterfall, game room, scuba, and jerk chicken everywhere you turn, I'd want to go to Jamaica, too. I'd be on that flight with Mom. But that's not the Jamaica that Mom flies to. No. When we go to Jamaica, we stay at my grandparents' home in hot, hot July. Not Ocho Rios. Brown's Town. Up in the hills with the goats, thunder and lightning every afternoon, and dumb cows in the street that stare into you like mind readers. We go to the Jamaica where cars zoom by at one hundred and thirty miles per hour, one-twenty if you're lucky. See, Robbie, you go to vacation-Jamaica. My mom takes us to the Jamaica where my cousins throw rocks at my 'baldie bean' because I don't have dreadlocks swinging from my head and I talk funny to them."

I guess I'm being loud, because the summertime library aide heads our way, trying to look older than the tenth grader she is. She puts her hands on her hips and says, "Boys," half singing, half warning us to lower the volume. We have nowhere else to draw, so we look sorry enough and she walks away.

"Hey," Robbie whispers. "I don't know what you're complaining about. That sounds cool. Adventurous. Like *Pirates of the Caribbean*. Well, except for the rocks. That must hurt."

I lean over, turn my head to show him the spot above the top of my ear. "Feel that." I lean even further.

"That's your skull, dude."

"Skull with a bump that'll never go down." He gives me the Brown's Town cow-in-the-street look. "Feel it," I order without raising my voice. The aide glances our way.

Robbie stretches across the table, places his hand on the spot, and feels around, but shakes his head no.

"I bled for days. Mom still calls it a little accident."

"Maybe it was."

"Whose side are you on?"

"I'm not taking sides."

Of course not. It's no secret Robbie has a crush on my

mom. I almost think he's drawing Pyra to look like her. It's time to talk about something else.

Being home with just Dad and me is great. Not that we do anything great. It's just great. Normal. Yeah. Normal. Dad sees his patients at the eye clinic, Robbie and I work on our epic comic strip showdown, and for dinner Dad and I feast on toast, pizza, franks, and Kung Pao chicken. We Skype with Colin, who not only cut off his dreads, he's shaved off all his hair and is now truly bald. Dad, Colin, and I crack jokes about his head shine and stuff and it's just great.

Then surprise! One night short of two weeks, Mom swings open the front door, rolling her luggage inside and bearing gifts, right in the middle of our daily Skype with Colin, who quickly disconnects the video call before she can see his newly shaved head. Mom's full of happy from her visit with the folks, and happy to be back home, and waits for Dad to go crazy over the bottle of dark Jamaican rum she brought him when Dad doesn't even like alcohol. At all. She whips out a bright yellow, black, and green cricket shirt she'll send to Colin, even though he'd left his cricket bat, gloves, and helmet in his room. Not too many cricket teams in Clemson, South Carolina.

Before she gives me whatever's in that bag for me, she

brushes my cheek, but her hand is so hot I jump.

"What's wrong with you, bwai?" she asks.

"You burned me," I say. "With your hand."

"Oh, Win. Don't be silly."

I touch my face. Pyra struck! "You did. You practically torched me."

She rolls her eyes and laughs it off. "Don't you want to see your gifts from your cousins?"

It's a trick question. The only answer is "no" because you know your cousins hate you, but of course I can't say "no."

"Sure."

She takes them out of the bag, one by one.

Holy jack-o'-lanterns in July.

They're coconuts. Carved, war-painted coconuts. Crazy-looking eyes, whittled straw hair, jagged mouths with glow-in-the-dark teeth, and high cheekbones. The one with the most hair has big flat teeth rising out of lips that are either smiling or hungry. The second coconut shows a full set of upper and lower teeth clenched tightly, its lips and carved nose pulled back in a sneer. The third coconut's mouth is wide open, revealing only three jagged teeth as if it had lost the rest tearing tree bark or animal flesh apart. Their eye pupils are painted the colors of fire; gold for the first, orange for the second, and blazing red for the third coconut head—all pupils swimming in black pools and shuttered by Day-Glo blue-and-pink eyelids. What they must look like in the dark! I don't even pick them up. The faces are too creepy to fake any thanks. Even worse, I feel the heat of her high beams on me. Her demented smile, waiting for me to make some kind of fuss over the demented coconut heads. Robbie would love her look. It's the look Pyra gets before she torches something. Someone.

"What's the matter?" she asks. "Don't you like them?"

"They're . . ." I don't know what to call them that won't make her flip out.

My father senses the flip is about to happen. He says, "Winston, why don't you put your gift from your cousins in your room while I get you"—he turns to Mom—"a frozen yogurt."

She nods to the frozen yogurt bribe.

I don't want to take the coconut heads, but I do. I take the creepy heads from her still-hot hands and hold them at arm's length, like they stink, and I run to my room and sit them on my bookshelf.

I look at them.

They look back at me.

They win. I turn their heads around so I won't have to see those faces.

*   *   *

It's too late to hide the carton of Kung Pao chicken. Mom dumps it in the trash and goes foraging in the meat freezer for cow's feet, and before you can say Bob Marley and the Wailers, she's chopping vegetables with a big cleaver.

Dad and I pass each other a look. Our vacation is over.

At dinner, Mom starts off the way she always does. Pleasant. But pleasant quickly disintegrates. "I expected a little more enthusiasm about your gifts, Winston. Your cousins made those especially for you."

I give her the Robbie shrug. "What they don't know won't hurt them."

She genuinely looks hurt, so I genuinely feel bad.

"With my own eyes, I see it, I see it." Uh-oh. Flippity-flop. "I never thought my own flesh and blood would be ashamed of the very people he comes from." She says "blood" with a small gasp at the end. Blood-*ah!* It's dramatic and embarrassing. What if I were to tell her Colin hacked off his dreads and shaved his head?

"Claudia," my father says.

Emboldened by two weeks of Kung Pao chicken, I speak up. "I'm not ashamed. I just don't think carved coconuts are gifts."

"Ungrateful. Disrespectful. Inconsiderate of the trouble

your own cousins go through for you. Rude. Plain rude-ah."

"Would they like it if I carved them a cantaloupe?"

Dad turns his stern voice on and aims it at me. "Winston."

"You don't know a gift when you see one," Mom says, and an image of those creepy coconut faces flashes before me. "Your cousins could have sold the set to wealthy tourists. That would have made a nice few dollars for them."

"They already *did* sell them to a wealthy tourist," my dad says—not that we're wealthy. We're not. Dad's joke is unexpected and we fist-bump.

"Go ahead. Make fun. Laugh," Mom says, and probably feels outnumbered without Colin at the table. "You didn't grow up as I did." She points her flame-throwing finger at me. "Your grandparents sacrificed for my education. Sacrificed." She looks at my father. "It's our fault, you know. Keeping him away from family and land."

And goats.

She does this. Brings up her waste not, want not childhood with the goats, the one school uniform for the year, the writing on both front and back sides of paper. I won't let her get me. I won't make a "sorry" face.

Later that night I'm thirsty. All I want is a tall glass of ice water and to fall asleep. I'm practically in the kitchen and

I stop at the entrance, careful to not make a sound. My mom is standing at the refrigerator, the freezer side open, her head resting on the side where the ice trays go. She almost looks headless with her neck and head shoved up in there.

I don't move. What do I say? Do? She doesn't hear me, or if she does, she doesn't stir. She just stands there with her head in the freezer. Sound like she's moaning or humming, but she doesn't hear me or sense I'm a few feet away.

Forget the glass of ice water. I back up slowly and tiptoe down the hall and into my room. I climb into bed and turn away from the bookshelf and my cousins' "gifts," even though they face the shelf's wooden backing. For luck I say prayers I haven't said since I was eight, then roll over to one side, then the other, and after doing that a few times, I fall asleep.

In the morning, when I open my eyes, three coconut heads stare at me from the bookshelf. I sit straight up.

At the library I tell Robbie what happened. How I turned the heads so I couldn't see their faces and how I woke up with their carved-out eyes staring me down. He doesn't believe me but wants to see the coconut heads. So I call Mom to ask if Robbie can come over for dinner and she says yes, which makes Robbie's day because he wishes he could ask her out. I tell him that's both sick and impossible. He counters with, "You mean like coconuts spinning around in the middle of the night?"

Before we sit down to eat, I take him to my room and show him the coconut heads. He practically shouts, loud enough for my mom to hear, "Those are cool!"

I glare at him. Traitor.

"They're better than what they sell in tourist shops. I like this one." He picks up the ugliest one by its straw hair. "Scary cool."

"That's nothing," I say. "Try waking up to them."

Robbie thinks I'm kidding. He runs his finger along the jaggedness of its open mouth, then traces the deep cheekbone carvings.

"Want them?"

He gives me the Brown's Town cow look.

I repeat myself. "Seriously. Do you want them? They're yours."

"Really?" He's happy like he's just won a prize. Then something changes in his face. He says, "I don't know," and sets the ugly coconut head down.

I laugh. "Not so cool, are they?"

Mom appears at my bedroom door. "Robbie's parents

taught him well. He knows not to take things that don't belong to him, like a family gift. And shame," she says, pointing her flame thrower at me. "Your cousins made those for you because they love and miss you, and yet you can't wait to give them away."

We're sitting at the table eating, hopefully changing the subject, but Robbie tries to score points with Mom.

"Oh, don't worry, Mrs. Bailey. I wouldn't take them."

"Because they're demented," I say. Dad waves both hands like an air traffic guy, signaling "no-fly zone."

"Demented?" Mom says. Her right eyebrow arches up. "Fine."

She pushes her chair back, gets up, and stomps down the hall. One door slams and then another. Her heels beat the floor. Then she sits back down. She's cool. Not crazy.

"Pass the rice and peas," she says calmly, like she didn't have a door-slamming fit two seconds ago.

Dad looks my way, like *Boy, I feel sorry for you.*

Robbie passes the dish to Mom and plunges the final stab in my back. "This stew is awesome, Mrs. Bailey. Better than the best restaurant in Montego Bay."

She becomes smiles and sweetness. "You really must see the whole country, Robbie, not just the tourist spots. You would love it." Her eyes are sparkling and he's eating it up. Then she turns to me. "At least someone knows what's good."

Robbie chomps on his beef stew like it's paradise on a fork. Dad refuses to throw me a rope. I'm on my own.

I try a piece of beef. I chew the meat.

Then, my tongue is beyond fire, like it's been skin-stripped and stabbed again and again. I drop the fork and spit the chewed beef onto my plate and bang the table with my fist. "WATER!"

"Son—" Dad says.

"Water!"

There must be peppers in here. Mom knows I don't like peppers. I'm coughing and dying, but she says in an even tone, "Water's right in front of you. And for heaven's sake, use your napkin!"

I don't care about the mess on my plate. I can't see. My tears are so hot I clamp my eyes shut.

"Dude, dude," Robbie says. My eyes are tearing and baking. I can't open them so I can reach for where I think my glass is. Hands, my father's hands, grab mine and my water glass before I knock it over. He puts the glass to my mouth and I gulp, which is worse somehow, as the fire spreads down my throat and invades my body.

"Get the boy some milk," he orders Mom. Either she's

moving slowly or time is stuck. I swear my tongue has swollen by the time she comes back with a glass of milk. I slurp it down, streams of white run down my face, and Mother says, "Really, Winston. If you just ate your food"—what she calls Jamaican food—"then you'd be able to pop peppers like you do movie popcorn. Now use your napkin."

In my head I remember that she ladled the stew onto our plates. That she always picks the Jamaican peppers out of my plate because only she, Colin, and Dad can eat them. She goes on chatting about pure, pleasant nonsense while my eyes still burn and I'm not done coughing. Robbie's under her spell. I'll bet there's no hot peppers in his stew.

That night I shower, text Colin about Mom and the madhouse, then click off the lamp. I'm almost to dreamland, but Mom isn't done with me yet. She stomps through the house like the fee-fi-fo-fum giant. I shut my eyes when I hear the thump of house slippers near my door. She enters and then *THWOK!* She bangs the three coconut heads on my dresser, mutters something angry and sinister I can't make out, then says, "Me get y'fatta next." She shriek-laughs and stomps away.

When it's safe, I peer up from the sheets into the dark. All I can see is the glow of white, blue, pink, and red paint on those crazy coconut heads. Their eyes seem to rise over high cheekbones and watch me. The faces, I swear, are in my cousins' likenesses. The coconut heads don't move, but their mouths are fixed to chomp or shriek. They're facing me, but I'm too whipped to get up to turn them around. I flop over on my other side.

I'm five or six years old. I'm in the center of a circle. There's singing. We're playing kindergarten games. Ring Around the Rosie.

That's not singing. It's chanting.

"Find a boy,
Hunt a boy,
We chop, chop, chop!"

Knives. Big knives. Machetes. Chopping.

I run. Mother says, "Silly bwai! Don't you know play when you see it?"

Cousins swing machetes, chanting, "We chop, chop, chop!"

I break out of the circle and outrun the chanting. Knees kick up high. I'm winning.

I look down. Tree trunks. My thighs and legs are massive

tree trunks. Coconut trees. I can't outrun the chanting.

Behind me. Slicing through the air. Machetes hacking. Goats bleating. Mother and cousins chanting:

*"Fee fi fo fum
Baldie bean
Ya bedda run!"*

I turn around and *whoosh!* I see the gleam of blades. *Whoosh-whoosh. Whoosh-whoosh.*

The shriek-laugh. The goats. And *whoosh!*

This is what I know. Your dreams will never kill you because you always wake up in time. I know this awake and I know this while I'm dreaming. When the blades come close enough to strike, my eyes pop open.

But instead of waking up alone in my bed, I am staring into the eyes of the coconut heads. On my bed. At my feet. Not on the dresser, where Mom left them.

Then I scream for real.

My mother comes running. She's in her white lab coat and not panicky like a mother checking on her poor son. She looks both satisfied and annoyed. "What do you mean by all of this noise in the morning? The neighbors think we're in here killing you."

I'm still catching my breath, but those were my thoughts exactly. I point to the coconut heads. I can't speak yet.

She glances at them, sighs, and turns to me. "I thought you didn't want them and now you can't sleep without them." She's playing dumb to torture me.

"I didn't put them on my bed," I say as strong as I can to my mother. "You put them there at the foot of my bed to haunt me."

"Haunt you, bwai? Don't be silly. Now get up and gather your clothes for laundry before you run to camp. And don't just throw the clothes into the wash. You separate them first, you hear me? And be quick. I have to open the office." Her teeth chatter like skeleton teeth. She cares more about the laundry than my near heart attack.

"Don't I get to eat first?" I ask, although I doubt I can eat breakfast or keep it down.

"I want your laundry in the wash before you leave. I'm seeing patients today. I don't have time to do everything."

She's about to leave, but I call out.

"Wait!"

She turns.

"Aren't you taking those things with you?"

"Make your mind up, bwai. You want them, you don't

want them. But you should want them, Winston. You should." I look down to the foot of the bed. They're more demented than the first time I laid eyes on them, their cheeks higher, their carved mouths hungry.

"Didn't you put them on my bed?"

She rolls her eyes up, sighs, and leaves me there, with those heads staring at me.

I sit up and stare them down. They stare back. They win.

I slide out of bed carefully and make my way to the closet without turning my back on them. The last thing I want is for them to take me by surprise. I keep the closet door wide open while I pull stuff out of my old toy chest until I come up with a "Go Joe!" camouflage blanket from back when I was collecting those action figures. I keep my eyes on the coconuts and creep up behind them, their backs still to me. I stand a little hunched, arms up, ready for the grab and run. Before they move, I suck in my breath, drop the "Go Joe!" camouflage blanket over them, drawing them together like pirate booty, and throw them into the toy chest. I slam and latch the lid, slam the closet door, and wedge the back of my desk chair under the closet knob. No way am I opening it again. If I have any dirty clothes in the closet, they'll have to stay dirty.

I grab the clothes from my hamper and don't bother to sort the whites from the colors. I throw everything into the wash, take my shower, dress while I'm still wet, and try to get far from those coconut heads. I'm almost out of my room, wet feet in sneakers, when I hear:

Chok. Chok-chok!

I scream. Not loud. But I scream.

Mom meets me in the hallway, her stethoscope hanging around the white coat's collar. "My staff will be here soon," she says. "What you screaming about now?"

"The noise," I say.

"Oh, Winston. Noise? What noise? The washer?"

"No. The heads!" I grab the chest piece to her stethoscope and place it over my heart. "Hear that? I'm not playing."

"No, dear. You're giving yourself a heart attack."

I start to tell her about the heads trying to escape from the toy box, but the doorbell to her office buzzes and she's rushing to get it.

She didn't even fuss about my wet shower hair. I'm in survival mode. On my own. When she returns from letting her receptionist in, I ask, "Can I sleep over at Robbie's?"

"Robbie can sleep over here," she says. "Now go to camp. I'm not driving you."

"Why can't I sleep over there?" I counter.

She says, "Because you broke his mother's lamp. The lamp from Budapest. The lamp her grandmother smuggled out of Hungary. You broke the lamp is why. Now run."

There is no way I am sleeping in my room. Ever. I catch up to Robbie and ask if I can sleep over. He says, "Dude. My mom won't let you up the front steps."

That's that. I don't bother to tell him about the heads that teleport from my dresser to the foot of my bed. If he didn't believe me the first time I told him about the heads, he won't believe me now.

I'm on my own.

Night comes too soon. I wait for my parents to turn out their lights, and I search for a safe corner in the house to hole up. Someplace where the coconut heads can't find me. Or, someplace where Mom can't find me.

She locks her office so there's no access to that part of the house, and deep down I know her office is the last place I should hide. I look inside Colin's room. It's almost empty, except for the furniture. He took the good stuff with him when he left for college. On top of his dresser sits the wooden cricket ball, his helmet, his gloves, and his cricket bat. I never got the hang of cricket. I just couldn't get into it. I hop onto his bed and settle in.

"Wish you were here," I tell Colin's room.
I fall asleep.

I can't see myself. I can't see where I am.
I hear chanting. It gets louder.

"We come for you,
We come for you,
Chop, chop, chop.
Chop, chop, chop."

I'm surrounded.
Cousins, Mom, Dad, Robbie become coconut heads, Pyra, cow, goat.
I know I'm dreaming the bad dream.
So I tell myself, "WAKE UP!"
The three coconut heads dance before my eyes.
I don't even scream. I run to the dresser, grab Colin's cricket bat, and swing it at the dancing coconut heads for life and death. Swing like they're hardballs until I make contact.
Cuck-CRACK!
I get one.
Then the other!

And the last coconut head is tricky, but I get him. Split him wide with the cricket bat and keep swinging and smashing.

I don't even hear my mother and father enter the room. That part's a blur. But I feel my father's hands taking the cricket bat from me. I feel the other touch on my forehead and neck and that touch is hot! Hot! Then cold.

I awake in a fog that slowly clears around me. I don't know what time it is or how long I've been out, but when I push myself out of bed and onto the floor, I barely feel my feet against it, like I'm wearing six pairs of thick socks. My ears slowly awaken to sound and I stumble toward it.

I make out two sounds. Two distinct sounds. One is a steady tapping or knocking. The other is my mother's voice. I feel clumsy but manage to creep toward the sounds, without making noise—or at least I can't hear myself making noise. I'm not sure I want her to know I'm up. When I hear words, distinct words, I stop and try to grab onto their meaning.

Chop, chop, chop, chop, chop.

She's in the kitchen. I rub my ears as if that would help me hear better. ". . . We had to sedate him." There is silence. The other person is talking.

I want to stick my head in to see my mother's expression, and at the same time I don't want to see her face.

It's her turn to talk. She says, "You know these kids. Their changes. Their stresses."

More from the other side. Then Mom says she can't take off any more days. Her patients have waited long enough for her to reopen the office. Silence. She says my dad can't take off either. Longer silence. She says, "I agree. Winston needs rest. Air. Clean air. Up in the country. Up in the hills. With his cousins. Yeah, mon."

My ears are now clear, and the cold from the floor creeps into my bare feet.

Something else is being said on the other side. Something that causes her to laugh. It's a short laugh. High-pitched. Shrieky. "So you'll come for him, eh? You'll come for the bwai?"

The cleaver hammers and doesn't stop.

Chop, chop, chop.

Chop, chop, chop.

MANIFEST
WORDS BY ADELE GRIFFIN
ART BY LISA BROWN

If I'd known what suffering Thaddeus Rolf would bring me, I'd have put an end to my life right then.

Instead, I took his.

For as long as I could remember, I had lived in virtual slavery to Mr. Bludmoore, who'd bought me as a young whelp from the London Foundlings Hospital and had worked me like a mule at his establishment, the Ruddy Duck, until my present age, thirteen.

The years had been kinder to Rolf, who could have been my well-fed, strapping twin. Appearing in the doorway of the Duck in his worsted suit and hob-nailed boots, the toff was quick to show me his shilling for supper and the papers in his pocket that I could not read, but that he boasted gave him passage on the *Charming Molly*, set to sail for America the very next day.

"Mother's dying wish was for her beloved brother, my uncle Würtemberger, to raise me as his own," Rolf informed the empty room as I served him a tin plate of trotters—I'd slaughtered, skinned, and hung the pig myself last week—along with a mug of red wine. "This is my last meal on dry land. We dock in Philadelphia, where there are already thirteen churches and a courthouse. Uncle is a cattle farmer outside the city proper. He's got his own dwelling, stables, and barns on the Schuylkill—and a king's feast on the table each night."

He spoke too of his dead father, "A sailor who went twice round the world. Pa's triumphs were tattooed on his body, before his ship sunk off the coast of Cape Horn. That's why I'm signed on as cabin boy. Uncle wanted to purchase the whole of my passage, but I'm born and bred a true sailor."

On and on boasted Rolf. Had my master not been out visiting Madame du Keating's fancy house that Sunday, he'd have clapped this ponce and sent him tumbling arse-over-teakettle into the night.

I myself had darker plans. Seeing that the young man was unused to drink, I kept his mug full as he kept on about his skills on the tennis lawn, his ability to understand the language of horses, his keen sense of smell. When he admitted he had no money for yet another, he offered to barter a bottle. "I'm an accomplished artist—I've got a pin-sharp eye for details." I gave him more drink in exchange for a charcoal sketch of my likeness.

"Grateful to you, mate. Pity you can't be my steward on the ship," slurred Rolf, his last words before he dropped his sketching coal and fell into a dead sleep. I lost no time. I hauled Rolf to the cellar, stripped him of his clothing and implements, stabbed him in the heart, then thrust his bloodied body, headfirst and still warm, into Master's barrel of stout, locking it fast and hiding the key. My last slaughter, I swore to myself. Bludmoore would have to enslave another soul to muck his stable and butcher his livestock.

Then I buttoned on my new worsted suit, checked my new pockets for my new papers of passage, and left.

I'd never been chancer, because I'd never had a chance. Now my future stretched in a tightrope before me. Straightaway, I put as much distance as I could between my crime and myself, not stopping until I'd arrived at the city's outskirts. I cowered under the wharf with other ragged folk, waiting out the black hours. Just before dawn, my cap set low, I completed the distance to London Port, where the *Charming Molly* was docked.

She was a beauty, with fore and main masts square-rigged, built of pale metal and copper fastened. She was my mistress and my salvation. I'd escaped my master's bull-whip, I'd dodged the hangman's noose, and if I succeeded in this journey, I might call myself free.

I could not write, so merely made an "X" on the ship's outbound manifest. The quartermaster inscribed the rest:

Thaddeus Elijah Rolf.

Over and done, with not a body on board to know that my face told a different tale than my name.

I'd found a net of horehound drops in Rolf's hold-all, and I struck up quick friendships by offering them around as I boarded the ship. I approached the ship's master, Captain Wright, with my most convincing manner. Wright accepted me on the spot—but it wasn't until the boat was towed out of the Catwater into the Sound, far away forever from Mr. Bludmoore and the Ruddy Duck, that I found I could breathe easy.

My new master was a man of few words, but he soon took a shine to me. There wasn't a job I wouldn't do: swabbie, rigger, chamber-pot emptier, mender, and message-deliverer. I was first on-deck by morn and last to my berth at night, never seasick, and hearty all day on my diet of fish if we caught any, tack if we didn't. The work was as brutal as any of my days at the Ruddy Duck, but there was fresh air, no whip, and the promise of a loving uncle at the end of the journey. It seemed, for a time, I could count myself lucky.

It wasn't more than a week passed before First Mate Endicott recommended promoting me to deckhand.

"A sailor without a tattoo is like a boat without anchor. Surgeon Clarke will ink you, so none will mistake you for a landlubber," Endicott said as he showed me the artistry that bound his own wrists. "I've got more than a few— each with its own meaning. Soon, you shall too. You're a fine young seaman, Rolf."

"Thank you, sir."

From above, I heard the mournful call of an albatross.

But now was not the time for guilt.

Late that evening, a squall blew up. Waves tossed the *Molly* so fierce that below-line was mayhem, souls wailing in fear and misery, among a tumult of falling crates and trunks. I joined the crew above-deck, working hard hours to fasten the battens. I was jolted awake in my berth before the sunrise to a sharp cry that I took for one of the frightened passengers.

But no, this cry was my own.

Blistering pain seared both my wrists—what dread

affliction was this? By dawn, I saw the truth of this horror—not boils, not some strange flesh-rot, but an intricate
tattoo of rope, the very image of Endicott's ink.

How had Surgeon Clarke kept me
sleeping as he performed the job? I
didn't feel drunk or drugged,
only weak with pain.

*for a
deckhand*

"Play your games,
Sawbones," I muttered as
I unrolled and buttoned my
cuffs. "I'll pay you no mind, and
you'll soon tire of them."

By midday, the swells had mod-
erated, the ship steadied course, and
while I was sure Clarke had marked
me for ill-use, I did not confront
him. I attended my duties, which
now included caring for the sick, as a dread out-
break of smallpox was the latest of the ship's afflictions.

Over the next days, three babies were lost, all quickly
committed to the deep, and soon sea burials became the
norm, as the pox was followed by a scourge of ship-fever
that took two more children's lives, along with Middy
Daniels and Surgeon Clarke himself, poisoned by the care

of his patients. Sailors began to mutter
of a curse on the ship.

for crossing
the Atlantic

By the fog of morning, I woke to a
smarting pain, as if a cat had clawed
at me all night; now my skin bore an
anchor on my right arm and a swallow on my left. I was becoming a
canvas of false boasts. How could
this be the surgeon's doing?
Clarke was dead and gone. This
had to be the work of a savage
spirit. My sleep, if it came at all,
was a torment, plagued by nightmares of a
cloven-hoofed creature rising up from the mist and snatch-
ing me down to a watery grave.

for 5,000
nautical miles
traveled

The ship was accursed—this was the whisper from crew to passengers, and it seemed most miserably proven when we learned that pretty songbird Jane Swiggum, the ship's favorite, had died of the ship-fever in the night. That morning, passengers stole onto the blustery deck for the reading and hymns.

With a heavy heart, I helped fellow deckhand Middy Boyd throw over the girl's mattress and bedding, then her wrapped body, into the dark Atlantic.

As the crew shepherded mourners back down to the safety below-deck, I felt a sudden stick of the needle, this time in my waking hours, at the core of my gut—and with this pain, a feverish revelation:

I am the curse of the Charming Molly.

"This storm might blow up to a gale by midday," called Endicott. "Rolf! Boyd! You'll need to repair the mainsail quick."

Even in wind and rain, I was nimble, and I climbed the rigging quick as a squirrel, but as I drew the mending needle through the cloth, the sight of it made me nauseated. I heard his voice: "I've got a pin-sharp eye for detail" and I could hardly get the job done before I descended all a tremble.

"By God!" Eyes wide in shock, Endicott stabbed his

finger at me—"What devil has possessed you, Rolf? Your arms are covered in—" before fate and the heavens opened, and in the next blustering wind, the boom came loose and swung around so hard it killed Endicott on the spot. In the havoc that ensued, my own pain intensified, my belly stung by a thousand hornets. I slunk below, leaving the others to dispose of Endicott's body.

"This ship's demon will be the end of us," muttered Old Pete that evening as he ladled me a supper of maggoty flour soup. His milky eyes rolled in their sockets. "I might have lost my sight, but that don't mean I can't feel its wrath."

for a voyage to China

I crawled to the fo'c'sle like a rat to its den, hiding from my captain, and spent the next hours wincing from the savagery that spread across my chest and belly. I could not see the mutilation, only, eventually, its result, rolling across my flesh in a myriad of greens and reds, a large dragon.

"Thaddeus Rolf," I whispered. "I know this is your handiwork."

Perhaps I always had.

Later, I stole back to the main berth, dug into my hold-all, and forced myself to extract Rolf's sketching pad. I might have left his body to pickle in a barrel of ale, but he was not done with me. Among his sketches, I now saw he'd drawn page upon page of tattoos, presumably intended for his own skin—designs I now wore. The final portrait was of Rolf himself, his eyes black as a goat's, his mouth twisted in mockery. I threw the drawings overboard and watched them float atop the swells until they were sucked under.

That night, as the ship bucked like a horse, I lay whimpering, for now it was my back shredded in agony. From shoulder blade to shoulder blade, a fully rigged ship—I knew this without having to see it in the cracked mirror of the captain's stateroom.

For the first

for travel around Cape Horn

time, I was too ill to leave my pallet.

"If it's the pox you've got, don't breathe on me," growled Boyd, soused with drink, delivering me with a bruising kick in the ribs from his hammock above.

But I did not die. Curled up in my berth, I was a helpless victim of the ghost infesting my skin. My body, no longer in rude and ruddy health, was now left to live or die with the other invalid emigrants. But after land was sighted, Captain Wright came below and informed us that the weakest would not be allowed off, but sent back to the Old Country. This was the final blow.

I had come too far. I would get off this ship, or die trying.

"Sir, I am much recovered," I called. My voice was ragged, my body so weak I could hardly stumble to a stand, and so I made myself crawl on hands and knees above-deck. In the light of a noonday sun I had not seen in weeks, my body was a tapestry of ink: a pig on my left foot and a rooster on my right,

for protection from drowning

a reminder to hold tight to the rigging

my knuckles scraped with letters, and a dagger in a jagged cut across my heart.

Old Pete was first to turn on me.

"Drown that one! Drown him like a rat!" he called. "It was the bounder, Thaddeus Rolf, who was the devil among us! Rolf, the curse of the *Charming Molly*!"

All able bodies seized me, hauled me bowside, and chucked me over the ship into the harbor. I was a London tavern boy who'd never learned to swim, and now, finally, the water had me in its power. The promise of death, that cold eternity to end my present sorrows, was as terrifying as it was intoxicating—until I could hear shouts from above, and my flailing hand knocked into a pole.

"Catch hold of the net, boy! Catch hold!"

I grasped and held, and was towed in to the dock,

for a fallen comrade

where I climbed the stiles, coughing, waterlogged, my brain a confusion and shock of what almost had been. A crowd had gathered dockside—to gape and gawk at my freakish markings, I assumed. But it seemed the sea had washed away my secrets.

Those who had seen, now only swore they had, but had to question their eyes. For not a single tattoo appeared on my skin.

"Thaddeus Rolf. You belong to me now."

There was no mercy in the hard face of my rescuer, whose hand still grasped the net that had reeled me in.

"Uncle?"

"Uncle . . . and master. Paid the captain for your passage, fair and square. There are papers to prove it. Whatever curse you brought onto that ship, I'll deliver a penance twice as harsh," declared Würtemberger. "It was my sister's wish you journey here, but not mine. From this moment on, you're a bound-out. You'll work in the slaughterhouse of my farm for the next seven years to square your debt with me. Are you listening, boy?"

Papers to prove it. Papers I could not read. I had journeyed ten weeks and over three thousand nautical miles, but I had escaped nothing.

From above, I heard the mournful call of an albatross.

DISAPPEAR!
BY R.L. STINE

My name is Mark Martindale, but my magician name is Magic Marko. Yes, I'm one of those weird kids who is totally into magic and magicians and tricks. Someday, I'm going to be a famous magician and amaze millions of people. I'm serious.

Magic can be surprising and puzzling. This story is about the day I discovered magic can also be *terrifying*.

My plan to be a great magician started when I was ten, and my uncle Andrew gave me a big suitcase filled with magic tricks. Uncle Andrew is my only fun relative. I have a ton of aunts and uncles, and whenever I see them, all they want to talk about is my height.

"Wow, Mark, look how tall you're getting!"

"Mark, you have grown so much since I saw you last time."

"Mark, you're going to be a basketball player. I know it."

Why are they always so surprised that I grew? Did they all expect me to *shrink*?

Andrew is my only uncle who never talks about my height. He and Aunt Laura live in Florida, so we see them only once a year. They always bring a huge crate of Florida oranges. I guess they think we can't get oranges here in New Jersey.

But they are totally cool. And two years ago when they came to our house, Uncle Andrew pushed this huge suitcase into my hands. "I had one of these when I was a kid," he said. "I spent hours and hours with these tricks. Bet you will, too."

"Wow, thanks!" I couldn't hide my excitement.

The front of the suitcase showed an old-fashioned-looking magician with a black mustache, a long black-and-red cape draped around his shoulders, and a tall shiny top hat on his head. He waved a magic wand in one hand, and the words *Presto Change-O!* were in a balloon pointing to his grinning mouth.

At the top of the case were the words: 100! MAGIC TRICKS! 100!

And at the bottom, in bold black type, it read: AMAZE YOUR FRIENDS! ASTOUND AUDIENCES! EASY TO PERFORM—IMPOSSIBLE TO FORGET!

"What's that?" My little brother Kevin bumped up between Uncle Andrew and me and grabbed the suitcase.

"Get off that!" I cried. His hands were wet and sticky from eating a Florida orange. "Look—you got sticky stuff on my magic case."

"So what?" He rubbed his hand on the case again and laughed.

Kevin can't help it. He's only seven. He's the younger brother, so he always wants whatever belongs to me, and he always tries to mess it up.

Yes, he's a pain. But Mom says my main job in life is not to get angry at Kevin. Even when he's a beast. She says my job is to take care of him.

Dad agreed with her. "Being the younger brother is a tough job, Mark," he said. "You wouldn't like it."

"But it's a tough job being Kevin's *older* brother!" I said.

For some reason, that made them both laugh.

"Let's take a look at what's inside the case," Uncle Andrew said. He helped me carry the big suitcase to the dining room table. "See if we can figure out some of the tricks."

"Can I do tricks, too?" Kevin asked. He stepped hard on my sneaker and tried to trip me. That's one of his favorite moves.

"Kevin, you have a very important job," I told him. "You will be the audience. That means you have to watch every move."

He nodded. He seemed okay with that.

Uncle Andrew had some trouble opening the case, but finally, the latch popped open, and we pulled up the lid. My eyes bulged when I saw all the trick supplies inside. Decks of cards, colored balls, ropes, handcuffs, wands, flowers, and even a stuffed rabbit.

Kevin grabbed for a set of little red balls, but I shoved his hand away. "You are the audience, remember?" I told him. "That's an important job."

I lifted a flat top hat from the the case and popped it with my fist. It snapped into place, tall and shiny. Then I removed a fake black mustache. I raised it to my nose.

"You don't need those," Uncle Andrew said. "Set them aside. That's too old-fashioned. Magicians don't look like that anymore."

I laughed. "What do magicians look like?"

"Like you," he said.

I pulled out a thick book. On the front, bold black letters

read: TOP SECRET! *For the Magician Only!*

"That's the instruction book," Uncle Andrew said. He took it from my hands and flipped through it. "You've got to be careful and hold on to this, Mark. It tells you how to do every trick from one to one hundred."

My heart was pounding. I don't know why I found this so exciting, but I did. Maybe I was *born* to be a magician. I didn't get this excited about sports. Or video games. Or cheeseburgers. Or *anything*.

"Let's try a trick," I said, gazing at the colorful equipment jammed inside the case. "We'll start with Number One. I'm going to learn them all, one by one."

Uncle Andrew laughed. I knew he wasn't laughing at me. He was happy that his gift was such a big hit.

I turned to Trick Number One in the instruction book. Then I pulled out three plastic cups with lids. I pulled off the lids. Each cup had a little red ball at the top.

"This is a disappearing ball trick," Uncle Andrew said, reading the instructions. "Put the lids back on. The next time you lift the lids, the red balls will be gone."

"Let me try it," I said. I glanced at the instructions. Then I placed the lids over the three balls. "Ready? Here goes," I said. "Watch carefully, Kevin."

I lifted the lids and the three balls had vanished.

Kevin let out a cry. "Good trick!"

Uncle Andrew and I exchanged glances. We both knew how the trick worked. It was totally easy.

"Hey—" I shouted to Mom, Dad, and Aunt Laura in the den. "I can do magic!"

"Show us," Mom called.

"Let's try Trick Number Two," I whispered to Uncle Andrew. "Find the ace of hearts in this deck of cards."

I pulled out the deck and shuffled through it. Every card in the deck was an ace of hearts. Awesome.

"Hold the deck upside down," Uncle Andrew said. "Don't let anyone see the cards."

I ran into the den to show off the card trick. "Hey, look. I'm going to try to find the ace of hearts in this deck. Shuffle the deck. Go ahead. Shuffle it as much as you want."

Everyone was totally amazed when I pulled out the ace of hearts.

And that's how I got hooked on magic.

From that day on, I spent all my spare time up in my room with the case of tricks. I was *obsessed*. I was crazed. I was nuts. I went through the instruction book, and one by one, I tried to learn all one hundred tricks.

At school, I brought in tricks and performed for my class. I did my Magic Marko act for the whole school at the annual talent show.

Word got around that I was a good magician. I started to perform at birthday parties for little kids and actually got paid for my act. I even did a magic act at *my own* birthday. My friends loved my card tricks and how I turned nickels into dollars and pulled quarters from their noses.

As I worked my way through the instruction book, the tricks got harder and harder to perform. But I didn't care. I loved it. I loved it so much I couldn't wait to get home after school and do magic tricks for *myself.*

So I'm sure you'll understand why I went out of my head, why I totally lost it, when I saw the big blue-and-yellow poster in the mall. I was walking to the shoe store with my dad, and there was the poster on the wall next to the Burger Barn. I saw the name *Alexander the Semi-Great* on it in huge letters, and my eyes blurred over.

"Dad, look—" I stopped walking and pointed with a trembling finger. "Alexander the Semi-Great is coming here. Check it out. It says he's giving shows at the Town Hall."

Dad had a paper coffee cup in his hand. He took a long sip from it as he squinted at the poster. "Who is he?"

"One of the greatest magicians on earth," I said. My chest felt all fluttery.

"Then why is he only *semi*-great?" Dad asked.

"He says it's important to stay humble," I told him.

"Dad, I have to see him perform." I tugged Dad's arm. In my excitement, I forgot about the coffee cup. It fell out of his hand and coffee splattered all over our shoes.

"That was a good trick," Dad said.

Sometimes he can say funny things.

I ran my finger over the poster. "Look. He's giving a show Saturday afternoon. You could drop me off. I have to go, Dad. I can't miss this. Seriously."

"Is he the guy who held his breath?" Dad said. "I think I saw him in a YouTube video holding his breath."

I nodded. "Yeah. Alexander the Semi-Great held his breath for two days straight."

Dad laughed. "And you believe that?"

"Some people think it was a trick," I said. "But I'm not sure." I tugged his sleeve again. "So can I go on Saturday?"

"Let's discuss it with your mother."

So here's how it ended up. They said I could go. They would drop me off at the Town Hall and then pick me up after the show. But I had to bring Kevin with me. And I had to *never* let Kevin out of my sight for a second. And I had to be nice to him no matter what he did.

Of course, I said yes to everything. I knew Kevin might be trouble. But there was no way I was going to miss this.

Kevin and I sat in the backseat as Dad drove us to the Town Hall. Kevin kept poking me hard in the ribs with one finger and then tickling me as hard as he could because he knows I hate it. He snapped my nose between his fingers, and he pulled my hair.

He was testing me.

I didn't crack. I didn't say one unkind word to him. I kept a smile frozen on my face, and as Kevin tortured me, I just kept picturing Alexander the Semi-Great onstage with me in the third row. Yes, our tickets were in the third row. I would be only *a few feet* away from one of the greatest magicians in history.

When Dad dropped us off in front of the theater, he gave me one more warning about taking good care of Kevin. I was too excited to answer. I took Kevin's hand and led him past the box office and into the building.

I had Kevin gripped in one hand and our tickets squeezed tightly in the other. Kevin kept trying to grab his ticket, but I kept it out of his reach. I knew if I gave it to him, he would drop it or lose it.

Town Hall is very old and dark and smells kind of sour. I stopped at the first aisle and gazed down the rows of seats. I saw a lot of kids with their parents, a lot of kids even younger than Kevin.

A dark red curtain stretched across the stage. Lights way up high in the domed ceiling cast a blue light over the theater. "This is the greatest day of my life!" I exclaimed to Kevin.

"Can I have popcorn?" he replied.

I bought him a *barrel* of popcorn. I wanted to keep him happy. Of course, he spilled half of it as we walked down the aisle to our seats. We were right in the middle of the third row. So close to the stage, I could almost reach out and touch Alexander the Semi-Great.

Was I excited? I had to *force* myself to breathe!

When the theater filled up and the blue lights started to dim, I gripped the arms of my chair so tightly, my hands ached. The show was about to start in a few seconds.

Kevin leaned toward me and put his mouth to my ear. "Mark, I have to go to the bathroom."

"NOT NOW!" I screamed. I couldn't help it. I lost it. Who wouldn't?!

"You promised Mom and Dad you wouldn't yell at me. I'm going to tell them."

"Kevin, please. The music is starting. Please," I begged.

"But I really have to go!"

I had no choice. I had to take him. I promised I wouldn't let him out of my sight for a second. He was ruining *everything* for me. But what could I do?

When we got back to our seats, Alexander the Semi-Great was already onstage. He was telling the audience that everything we'd see today was real. Real magic.

My eyes nearly popped out of my head. There he was. Right in front of me. He wore a shiny satin purple tuxedo, a white shirt, and a purple bow tie. His boots were purple, too, and came up nearly to his knees. Alexander had long, wavy black hair down past his shoulders, and black eyes that caught the stage light and appeared to glow.

I was so crazed, I stared at him without hearing a word he was saying. When he lifted off the floor, floated a foot above the stage, I gasped out loud like most everyone else in the audience.

"Everyone has the ability to float," Alexander announced. "It's all a matter of mind power. You need to open up the flight hemisphere of your brain—and you can float, too."

I squinted hard. Were there strings attached to him? Thin cords lifting him off the stage floor? I was sitting close enough to see that there was nothing above his head.

I lowered my eyes. Was he standing on a mirror to make it look as if he was floating? No. He floated to one side of the stage, then back, his arms lifted above his head.

"Many have tried this trick," he said. "But they all failed. Because this is not a trick!"

Then he lifted himself higher and did a somersault in the air. The audience went nuts, screaming and cheering and clapping. I went nuts, too.

I turned to Kevin, my heart pounding. "Do you believe it? Is that *awesome*?"

He nodded but didn't say anything. He *couldn't* say anything because his mouth was full of popcorn. He had popcorn butter smeared all over his cheeks.

The music soared as Alexander lowered himself to the stage. A woman came stepping onstage in a sparkling blue skirt and top. She had blond hair and very red lips, and she did a dance step as she moved toward Alexander.

"Such a beautiful young woman!" Alexander declared. "Too bad I'm going to make her disappear." The woman did some more dancing, then came to a stop beside him.

"Most magicians would have her step into a box and then disappear," Alexander said. "But everyone knows that's a trick. I don't do tricks. She's going to disappear— for real—and you can watch."

He reached into a bucket on the stage and dug both hands deep into it. Then he held up both fists, filled with something that looked like confetti. "When I drop this over her, she will disappear forever!"

He raised his fists over the young woman's head. Then he opened his hands and the confetti came flying down. "Disappear!" he cried.

She screamed—and disappeared. The confetti sprinkled silently over the stage floor.

The audience was quiet for a long time. I guess the whole thing was kind of a shock. Then we all cheered and clapped and went berserk.

And that's when I got a crazy idea. I needed to go backstage and talk to Alexander the Semi-Great.

I had twenty thoughts at once. Fireworks were exploding in my brain. At least, that's what it felt like.

This is what I was thinking:

I'm a magician, too. Maybe Alexander would like to meet a young magician.

Maybe Alexander would have some advice for me.

Maybe if I begged him, he'd tell me if he really can make people disappear.

I know that's a totally weird thought. But if you sat in the third row and saw that woman vanish right before your eyes, you would want to know if it was a trick—or if it was real.

Alexander finished his performance by diving into a huge glass tank of water and holding his breath for twenty minutes. I could tell he really wasn't breathing. I was close enough to see there were no air bubbles coming from his mouth or nose.

The audience gave him a standing ovation, cheering and screaming for at least ten minutes. Then everyone started to move down the aisles to leave the theater.

"Let's go," Kevin said, tugging my arm with sticky popcorn fingers.

"Wait," I said. "I have an idea." I didn't tell him what I planned to do. I knew he'd whine and complain and say we had to go home.

I pushed my way through the crowd to the front of the theater. I stopped at a narrow gray door by the side of the stage. "This must be the stage door," I told my brother.

"What are we doing?" he demanded. "Mom and Dad are waiting in the car."

"It will only take a minute," I said. I grabbed the handle and pulled the door open. My chest suddenly felt as if a million butterflies were fluttering in there. Was I really going to introduce myself to one of the greatest magicians of all time?

I stepped inside. Very dark back here. I could see a lot of sound and lighting equipment on the side of the stage. There were cables and wires everywhere. Down the long hall, I saw some rooms at the back. Probably dressing rooms.

It was hot back here, and the air smelled like sweat. I kept swallowing, trying to fight my nervousness. "Follow me," I whispered to Kevin.

But a big man, tall and very wide, with a stubby brown beard and a wool cap pulled over his head, stepped in front of us. "I think you boys went the wrong way," he said, hands on the sides of his gray uniform. "The exit is that way." He pointed.

"I . . . I . . ." My voice broke. "I'm a magician," I said. "I just wanted to shake hands with Alexander the Semi-Great."

The man scratched his forehead through the wool cap. "You're a magician?" He studied me.

"Well . . . kind of," I said.

For some reason, that made him laugh. "Okay. Go ahead. Alexander is in the basement, putting his stuff away." He pointed to a metal stairway. "Be careful, guys. He might turn you into rabbits."

He stepped aside so Kevin and I could walk to the stairs. Our shoes clanged on the metal rungs. Each clang made my heart skip a beat.

It's happening. I'm actually going to meet Alexander.

The stairs led down to a big supply room. I squinted in

the bright yellow light. I saw a row of dark lockers along one wall. Wooden crates were stacked against another wall. A pole of stage lights tilted against the crates.

"I don't see anyone," Kevin said. "Let's go. I don't like this place."

"You're not scared, are you?" I demanded.

"Of course not."

I knew that would shut him up.

I heard a cough. It came from a doorway at the end of the lockers. "Let's go." I tugged Kevin toward the door. My legs were trembling, but I couldn't let my brother know how tense I was.

Another room was filled by a long table. There were folding chairs all around it. I saw a tray of small potato chip bags on one end. And at the other end, a bald man sat forking up a salad from a large plate. He wore a black T-shirt and white basketball shorts. He looked up in surprise as Kevin and I burst in.

"Oh. I'm s-sorry," I stammered. "I'm looking for Alexander the Semi-Great."

He swallowed a mouthful of lettuce. "I'm Alexander," he said softly.

And then I saw the pile of long, black hair in front of him on the table. *Alexander wears a wig.*

"I . . . just wanted to meet you," I choked out. My pounding heart had jumped into my mouth. "I'm a magician, too."

"That's nice," he said. "But I'm busy. I'm eating my dinner." He tilted the bowl of salad so I could see it.

"I'm sorry," I said, backing up. "I just . . . well . . . I do tricks, too, and—"

"I don't do tricks," Alexander replied. "Everything I do is real."

I blinked. "I know. But . . ." I didn't know what to say. This wasn't going the way I planned it. I thought he'd be friendlier. "But you don't really make people disappear, right?" I blurted out.

He banged the table with his fist. "Of *course* I do."

I stared at him. "That woman on the stage . . . the one you dropped the confetti on. That wasn't a trick?"

He shook his bald head. "Not a trick. Want me to show you?"

My mouth dropped open. "You'll do it right now? For me?"

My legs were so wobbly, I could barely stand up. Alexander the Semi-Great was going to do a magic trick *just for me.*

He pushed his chair back and walked over to us. He had

beads of sweat on his bald head and a shred of lettuce stuck to his front tooth. He wiped his mouth with the palm of one hand. "What's your name, kid?"

"Mark. But my magician name is Magic Marko."

"Haha. Very clever." He didn't mean it. "Listen, Magic Marky, I can do the disappearing thing. But do you have any money?"

I made a gulping sound. "Money?"

He nodded. "This theater pays lousy. How much do you have on you?"

I reached my hand into my jeans pocket and felt the twenty-dollar-bill Dad gave me in case of an emergency. "Well . . . I have twenty dollars," I said.

"Okay." He reached out his hand. "Give me the twenty and I'll make someone disappear before your eyes."

I hesitated. This was definitely weird. I was going to pay Alexander twenty dollars to perform a trick? It didn't seem right, but I couldn't resist. I handed him the twenty.

He crinkled it up and stuffed it into the pocket of his shorts. "Okay," he said. "Watch very carefully. See if you can spot the 'trick.'"

He picked up a bag of potato chips from the food tray. He ripped the bag open. Then he dumped the chips over Kevin's head. "Disappear!" he shouted.

Kevin made a *yelp* sound and disappeared.

I uttered a cry. Kevin was gone. The air felt cold where he had been standing. I was kind of in shock. I couldn't move. I had to force myself to breathe.

Alexander grinned at me. "Did you see how I did that?"

I shook my head. "No."

He chuckled. "That's because it's not a trick. I really made him disappear."

He crinkled up the potato chip bag and tossed it on the floor. "Listen, kid, I've got to go. I promised I'd be somewhere. Nice meeting you."

He stepped past me and headed to the door.

"Hey, wait—" I called. "What about Kevin?"

He turned. "Was that his name? I made him disappear."

"I know," I said. "But where is he? We have to meet our parents out front."

Alexander shrugged. "Beats me. I don't know where he is. I made him disappear. I told you, dude, it wasn't a trick."

A cold chill made my whole body shake. "No. Wait," I said. "You . . . you're really scaring me. I need my brother. I'm in charge of him. I promised I'd take good care of him."

Alexander shrugged again. "Kid, you paid me twenty dollars to make him disappear. What do you want me to do?"

I felt sick. I struggled to keep my lunch down. *This isn't happening.*

I started to shout my brother's name. "Kevin! Kevin? Are you here?"

Silence.

"That won't help, kid," Alexander said. "He's disappeared."

That's when I lost it. "Well, bring him back!" I shouted. "Bring him back *now*! Do you want another twenty dollars? I can get more money from my parents. I'll pay you. Really."

Alexander sighed. "Tell you the honest truth, kid. I don't know how to bring them back. I only know how to make them disappear."

Another chill shook my body. "No . . . no way . . . ," I murmured. "He's my brother." And before I realized it, I burst into tears.

"Okay, okay." Alexander came hurrying over. "I'm just messing with you, kid. Guess I have a weird sense of humor. I'll get your brother. Just don't cry, okay? You'll get me into trouble."

He searched through the bags of potato chips and pulled one out. He tore the top off the bag, raised it high in the air, and spilled the chips onto the floor.

I blinked. Kevin stood in front of me, eyes wide with confusion. His face was crinkled up, like he didn't know where he was. "What was *that* about?" he said.

"You're okay!" I cried. I was so happy to see him, I almost hugged him. I rubbed the tears off my cheeks.

Then I turned to Alexander. "You're really mean," I said. "You shouldn't do that to people. You scared me to death."

He grinned. "I know. It's just a strange thing about me. I can't explain it. I like upsetting people and I really enjoy messing with their minds." He stared down at me. "No hard feelings?"

"No hard feelings," I said. I picked up a bag of potato chips and tore it open. Then I dumped the bag over Alexander's head. "Disappear!" I shouted.

Alexander the Semi-Great disappeared.

"Let's go," I told Kevin.

Kevin's mouth dropped open. "Huh? Mark? How'd you do that?" he asked.

"Easy. I read the front of the chip bags," I said. I held one up. "Look."

He read the front of the bag out loud: "*Vanishing Chips.*"

Kevin picked up another bag. The front said: *Reappearing Chips.*

"It's a real easy trick—if you have the chips," I said. I

tossed the bag onto the table.

"Are you going to bring him back?" Kevin asked.

I grinned at him. "I don't think so."

I put my arm around Kevin's shoulder and led him out of the room. "We'd better hurry. We're late."

We hurried up the stairs and out of the theater. Mom and Dad were waiting in the car. Kevin and I climbed into the backseat.

"Mark, how was the show?" Mom asked.

"Awesome," I said.

THE MANDIGORE
BY CLAIRE LEGRAND

Grandma Ruby had never trusted libraries.

"Don't go," she told Clark one gray day, when he was twelve years old and in the seventh grade, and quite frankly hating life at the moment. It was Mrs. Lundgaard's fault. She was his history teacher, and she had assigned him a twenty-page paper on the Industrial Revolution for his end-of-semester project.

Nina got to write a paper on the Civil War, which was so much easier and more interesting—and also bloodier.

"Don't go where, Grandma?" Clark said, shoving a wrapped peanut butter sandwich into his bag. If he was going to be stuck at the library all day, he needed provisions.

"To the library."

Clark tried not to roll his eyes. Dad said they had to be patient with Grandma Ruby. "I have to go. I have this stupid paper."

"Bad idea. It's a bad idea."

"Yeah, I think so, too. You shouldn't have to write research papers on the weekend. It should be illegal."

"In the dark, the rabbits wait
Hide their bellies, hide their eyes
In the dark, the rabbits run
Slit their bellies, slice their eyes . . ."

Grandma Ruby rocked in her chair, whisper-singing. Clark shivered, even though he had heard Grandma Ruby sing like this hundreds of times. Dad said she had been sick ever since Clark's aunt Mara died. Well . . . "died." It was the sort of thing where Aunt Mara disappeared one day and they hadn't ever been able to find her. Eventually they'd declared her dead, and there had been a memorial service. So the family could move on, that sort of thing.

Clark had never met Aunt Mara; she'd only been around his age when it happened. She'd been the baby of the family, the little princess, the youngest of five.

And then, one day, she was gone.

Grandma Ruby had gone looking for her, Dad said, even though everyone kept telling her not to. "I can find Mara," Grandma Ruby had insisted. "I know I can. She's my baby girl." So Grandma Ruby had left one night, while Grandpa Jim had been sleeping. Weeks later, after the police and the state troopers and even the FBI had been out looking for her and Mara, she'd come back.

Ever since that day, when Grandma Ruby came stumbling into the house with her eyes glassy and vacant, her hair tangled with twigs, her clothes stained with mud, she had been . . . different.

Sometimes she sang songs, and not the kind of songs you'd usually think about grandmothers singing.

"In the dark, the wolves are waiting
In the dark, the trees say run
The trees taste fear, the trees see blood
The Mandigore, he'll find you
The Mandigore, he smells so sweet . . ."

Grandma Ruby looked like she might cry, but she never did. Clark and his parents had to give her these eyedrops constantly, because she hardly ever blinked.

225

"Grandma, are you going to be okay?" Clark made Grandma Ruby look at him. "I really need to go. Mom's at the store. Dad's upstairs. He's working, but you can always ring the bell. Okay?"

Clark placed Grandma Ruby's hand on the bell attached to her wheelchair. She seized Clark's hands, gripping them hard enough to hurt.

"Don't go," she pleaded. "Mara said don't go."

"Grandma. Mara's dead."

"In the dark, Mara waits
Hides her belly, hides her eyes
The Mandigore, he has a crown
The Mandigore, he wants a treat . . ."

Clark left Grandma Ruby there, singing to herself. He didn't have time to listen to her weird songs. And he hated it when she sang about Aunt Mara. It made him think of Aunt Mara, twelve years old, just like him, hiding somewhere. Afraid. Waiting.

Twenty minutes later, Clark banged on Nina's beat-up screen door. He tried to ignore the overflowing mailbox and the sound of Nina's dad yelling at Nina's brothers.

Nina's dad was always yelling these days. Nina said he never used to, before he'd lost his job.

When Nina finally appeared, her eyes were red and her cheeks were wet. "*What?*"

"Why are you crying?"

Nina rubbed her face dry and came out onto the porch. "I'm not."

Clark grinned. "You were watching last night's episode again. Weren't you?"

"No."

"You totally were."

"All right, *all right*. I've watched it *five times* this morning. Are you happy?"

"Yes. You're even more obsessed than I am."

"So? Who cares? You're supposed to be obsessed with *Noctiluca*. That's why shows like that *exist*. So we can obsess over them."

Noctiluca was this sci-fi show. It was kind of like a space opera, with an evil government and rebels and epic battles and romance (which Clark said he didn't care about, but, in fact, he was totally rooting for Gertie May, the folksy engineer, and Nathaniel Vandeventer, the snooty doctor, to get together), except instead of it taking place in outer space, it was set in this underwater world. Kind of like the lost city of Atlantis, but with hundreds of cities instead of just one. The main cast was a motley crew of thieves with hearts of gold. *Noctiluca* was the name of Captain Farriday's subship. It glowed underwater, like a bioluminescent jellyfish.

Clark had been the new kid at his school this year. His family had moved to the island from the mainland to get away from the old house, where the family had been living when Aunt Mara disappeared. Clark's dad was hoping maybe this would help Grandma Ruby, who was getting worse.

"It'll help her to get away from old, bad memories," Clark's dad had explained. Which was all well and good, but it's not like Clark's dad had to deal with being the new kid at school.

On his first day, Clark had seen a poster on the cafeteria bulletin board—a poster for a *Noctiluca* fan club, which met after school on Thursdays in the auxiliary choir room.

Clark decided to go, even though part of him thought it might be a bad decision, socially. He had never talked to anyone about his love for *Noctiluca*. He wrote stories about *Noctiluca*, collected the DVDs and comics, and watched cast interviews on YouTube. But he never *talked* about it. Not until that first Thursday, when he went to the auxiliary choir room (which was more like an oversized closet) and met Nina.

"Marry, kiss, kill," Nina had said immediately. "Gertie May, Commander Talia, Captain Farriday."

"Um. Hi? My name's Clark."

Nina had glared at him. "Answer the question. Marry, kiss, kill."

"Um . . . okay. I'd marry Gertie May. Because you can't kill her. It'd be like killing a puppy. And I wouldn't want to kiss her because . . . well, that'd be mean to Dr. Vandeventer. Because he loves her."

Nina had nodded solemnly. "Continue."

"Kiss Commander Talia because . . ." Clark had blushed. "Well, because she's hot."

"Agreed," Nina had said. "I'm dressing up as her for Halloween. Just FYI."

"Okay . . ."

"And why would you kill Captain Farriday? That's pretty harsh."

"Because he would want me to. Because he'd rather die than have any of his crew get hurt. They're like his family. He'd do anything for them."

Nina had stood up to shake his hand. "Congratulations. You've passed the test. You're now officially part of the

Noctiluca fan club. Let's get started."

"Shouldn't we wait for everyone else?"

Nina had laughed. "Dude. Clark, right?"

"Yeah."

"Usually it's just me reading fan fiction in here. Alone. Do you actually think anyone else at this stupid school is smart enough to recognize the genius of *Noctiluca*?"

"Um . . . no?"

"Right. So let's get started. You can be vice president."

That's how Clark and Nina met. Eight meetings of the *Noctiluca* fan club and eight weekend *Noctiluca* marathons later, they were best friends. Clark gave Nina a pack of special edition *Noctiluca* trading cards for her birthday. She never went anywhere without them. Nina drew these *Noctiluca* comics for Clark, in which Captain Farriday looked suspiciously Clark-like, only if Clark were older and less gangly-looking. The comics were Clark's favorite thing in the world.

Nina was the only person Clark had told about Grandma Ruby's songs, and her fear of libraries.

Nina thought Grandma Ruby would make a great character on *Noctiluca*. Someone who knew the government's secrets, but had gone through so much torture her mind was screwed up, and you had to decipher her creepy songs to discover the truth.

"Come on, crybaby," Clark said to Nina. "Come with me to the library before it starts raining. We've got to finish our papers."

"I don't want to. I want to watch it again. So, did you cry when Gertie and Dr. V finally kissed?"

"No." Except Clark had, all over his popcorn. He was glad he and Nina had this policy to watch new episodes alone, and to only watch it together when they were both ready to share the emotional experience.

"You totally cried."

". . . Maybe a little."

Nina grinned. "You big softie."

They rode their bikes to the library because it was mid-November and pretty soon it'd be too cold on the island to ride bikes. Even now, the wind was biting and salty, so cold it stung. The sky was full of thick, dark clouds that looked like fists.

Nina rode ahead of Clark, because she always liked to be first, and Clark let her, even though her creaky bike was a million years old and Clark could have totally beaten her if he'd wanted to. But this way he could fall back and watch her dark hair flow in the wind like an ebony banner. This way he could think cheesy, bad-poetry things about Nina's hair, and imagine himself to be as handsome and smart as Dr. Vandeventer, and no one would ever know.

By the time they got to the library, the storm had hit.

They locked their bikes, ran inside, and stood in the lobby, dripping rain on the rug. Clark wished his reflection in the glass door didn't look so awkward.

A man hurried over with some towels. He was youngish, with those thick-rimmed glasses that made you look stylish in a nerdy kind of way, the kind Clark could never pull off. The man had messy brown hair, the kind of messy Clark knew girls liked.

Clark hated the guy on sight.

"Well, hello!" the man said to Clark. "I'm Mr. Dunn. I'm the librarian here. I didn't think anyone else would come today because of the weather."

"We can leave if you want," Clark said. "In fact, maybe we should—"

"Don't be stupid, we have to finish our papers." Nina took a towel from Mr. Dunn and smiled. "Thanks, Mr. D."

Mr. D? "You know him?" said Clark.

"Nina is one of our regulars," Mr. Dunn said, handing Clark a towel.

Clark took it, but he wasn't happy about it. "A regular?"

"She's a big fan of our graphic novels section. The *Noctiluca* collection in particular. Checks out a stack every weekend."

Clark turned to Nina. She wasn't looking at him. "But Nina, I thought you had all the *Noctiluca* comics. You keep them under your bed because they'll be worth something someday. You said—"

"Yeah, well, I lied, okay? I don't have money to buy all those books, Clark. Don't be stupid."

Nina stalked off into the stacks.

Clark watched her go. He knew Nina's dad hadn't worked in a long time, and that Nina's mom worked two jobs, and that Nina had three brothers. He knew all that, but he hadn't really *thought* about it until now, and what it really meant for Nina, and that made him feel like an idiot.

"I'm sorry," Clark mumbled, his cheeks burning, but Nina was too far away to hear.

"Well! Let me know if you need anything," said Mr. Dunn, his hands in his pockets. He smiled down at Clark. The overhead lights glinted off his glasses, making it hard to see his eyes.

Clark frowned, shoved the wet towel at Mr. Dunn. He felt rebellious, a little like *Noctiluca*'s rough-and-tumble mercenary, Jones. He shrugged off his wet coat, left it on the floor. Made his way to a table and sat and opened his notes and stared at them. A clock on the wall ticked through thirty minutes. An hour. He wondered where Nina had gone.

Thinking of Nina made his chest feel too tight to breathe.

Then he heard laughter—Nina's laughter. And someone talking to her—a deep, male voice. Mr. Dunn.

Clark gripped his pencil so hard it snapped in half.

And that's when he saw it. Right then, when his thoughts were roiling in his mind like the storm clouds outside. Right then, as he was imagining himself to be older, more muscular, cooler—like Dr. Vandeventer. Maybe even like Captain Farriday, who always knew just the right sarcastic, funny thing to say.

That's when he saw the kid with the fangs.

It was this flicker in the corner of Clark's vision, like when you get something stuck in your eye.

But it wouldn't go away, and it started to take shape—a skinny, pale figure. A boy, he thought. Two glowing eyes through a mask. Some kind of creature-mask, an animal. Sharp ears and a snout. Fangs. Arms and legs too long for its body, like someone had stretched him out. Crouching in the shadows, peeking around the corner of the nearest bookshelf.

Clark froze, this figure caught in his peripheral vision.

Then he snapped his head to face the boy, and the boy disappeared, like he had never been there in the first place. A shadow flickered across the tables, fast, and then darted up the bookshelves toward the ceiling, and then was gone.

It was like one of those tricks of the eye, when you see random shapes float behind your eyelids, and when you chase them, try to follow them, they fly away.

Clark stared, not blinking, not breathing, waiting for the boy to come back. At least, he was pretty sure it had been a boy. There came a series of clicks, like a wild animal speaking to its pack. Clark tried to follow the sound. He peeked behind the nearest bookshelves, climbed onto the table so he could see higher up. But nothing was there. He was alone. Everything was quiet, except for the rain hitting the roof. Everything smelled like books.

"Nina, I saw something."

Nina did not look up. She stared hard at the computer, writing furiously in her notebook. She was sitting by the wall farthest away from the windows, where the shadows were thickest. To Clark's eyes, they seemed to crawl, as if they were full of invisible, wriggling things.

"Nina, listen to me."

Nina ignored him.

"*Nina.*" Clark ripped her notebook away. "You're not even paying attention to what you're writing. You just wrote ten lines of scribbles."

Nina raised an eyebrow. "Your point?"

"Look. I saw something."

"Me too, Clark. I've seen lots of things. It's what eyes are for."

"I'm serious, Nina. There was this kid, okay? But he was wearing a mask, and he had fangs, and then when I tried to look right at him—"

"Is everything all right, kids?" asked Mr. Dunn, appearing out of nowhere. One minute, it was just Clark and Nina in the glow of the computer—and then, the next minute, Mr. Dunn was there, his hands in his pockets, smiling. The light from the computer reflected off his glasses. Clark couldn't see his eyes.

"We're fine, Mr. D," said Nina. "Clark's just being annoying. He's distracting me while I work. He claims to be seeing things."

Clark wanted to shake Nina. She could talk for hours about subships and deep-water parasites and whether or not Commander Talia used to work for the Company, but she wouldn't take him seriously *now*?

Mr. Dunn chuckled. "Seeing things, huh? Seems a bit early in the day for that. You haven't even been working for that long."

"It's nothing," Clark said. He wanted Mr. Dunn to go away. More specifically, he wanted Mr. Dunn to shrivel up into nothing, to never have existed. If Mr. Dunn hadn't talked about Nina and the *Noctiluca* graphic novels, Clark would never have made Nina mad, and they would be working together right now, and maybe they would share Clark's peanut butter sandwich while reading *Noctiluca* fan fiction on Clark's phone. Maybe she would scoot closer to him while they read.

"He says he saw a kid. With *fangs*." Nina shook her head. "A kid with fangs and a *mask*. I think he's trying to scare me. Which, yeah, good luck with that, Clarky. I'm not the one who had nightmares for days after watching 'Waylaid.' I'm not the one who still, to this day, has to watch that episode with all the lights on." Nina looked up, her eyes flashing. "Isn't dat wight, wittle Cwarky?"

Clark found himself caught between twin urges—the urge to melt into a puddle, seep into the floor, and be gone forever; and the urge to yell and scream and kick the table until Nina stopped making fun of him.

That's when he saw it for the second time:

The kid with the fangs, and the mask, and the too-long limbs. Hovering in the shadows underneath the "Read" poster featuring Sir Patrick Stewart.

Clark held his breath, keeping the masked, fanged kid in the corner of his eye. The longer he waited, the clearer the kid became. It wasn't a boy this time. It was a girl.

"A kid, huh?" Mr. Dunn said, and Clark blinked, startled, and the girl at the edge of his vision was gone. A shadow raced through the darkened room, zipped between chairs, bled up the wall in a black patch. It hovered near the ceiling, like the shape of something too far beneath the water to see clearly.

"Tell me about this kid," Mr. Dunn was saying. "What did he look like?"

Clark tried to speak, but his throat was scratchy. He couldn't stop staring at that dark spot on the ceiling. "What do you mean?"

"I mean exactly that. What did he look like, this kid you saw?"

Nina rolled her eyes. "He had *fangs*! He was wearing a *mask*! Go away, Clark. Go write your paper."

"He moved really fast," Clark said, ignoring Nina. The

room was too dark. The shadows sat thickly on his skin. He wanted to brush them off, like cobwebs. He wanted to turn on all the lights. "At first I just kind of saw him out of the corner of my eye, but then . . ." Clark stopped talking. It sounded stupid, said out loud.

"Yes? What then? Tell me." Mr. Dunn's hands were still in his pockets. The computer light still shone off his glasses.

He seemed taller now, even though he hadn't moved an inch.

He licked his lips.

Clark tried not to stare. Maybe he was going crazy. Quite possibly he was sleep-deprived. "Nothing. I don't know. I don't remember. It happened really fast."

"Of course. I understand." Mr. Dunn smiled. "Libraries do funny things to the brain, I've found. Especially on gloomy days like this. Anyway, I'll be at the reference desk if you need me."

Once Mr. Dunn was gone, Clark turned to find Nina staring at him.

"What? Are you about to yell at me some more?"

"No," she said. "I was just thinking you might be right."

"About *what*?"

"About the kid with the fangs." She swallowed. "I think I just saw him, too."

*　*　*

Clark and Nina huddled beside each other in front of the computer, pretending to work.

"You're sure you saw him?" whispered Clark.

Nina exhaled slowly. "I think it was a girl, actually. I was thinking about how mad you were making me, how dumb you were acting. I figured you were trying to distract me from being mad at you by pretending to see things. I felt so mad I wanted to punch something. That's when I saw her."

Clark decided to skip the part about Nina being mad at him. "We can't both be seeing things, can we?"

"I don't think so. One person hallucinating, sure. Two people hallucinating *different* things, okay. But two people hallucinating the same exact thing?"

"You could be lying, I guess. Pretending you saw exactly what I saw, just to freak me out."

"Clark. Do you remember, in 'Sub Zero,' when Jones and Gertie May were stuck underwater in their suits, trying to make that engine repair, and Gertie May's suit was running out of air, and Jones told her he'd save her, no matter what? He kept promising her, over and over, that he would save her. He *swore* he would. He swore on his favorite gun."

Clark nodded. It was the first episode that had made

him cry, because it was when he'd realized mean old Jones-y actually had a heart.

Nina started speaking in a fairly decent Jones accent. "I swear to you, Clark—I swear it on Clementine's precious metal life—" Nina made a motion like Jones cocking his gun. "*I am not lyin' to you.*"

Clark tried to smile. "Well, so what do we do about it? Should we just leave? What do you think it means?"

"Actually," Nina said, talking like Nina again, "I was thinking about your grandmother."

"Grandma Ruby?"

"I was thinking about the songs she sings. I don't know why. I just always think about her when I go to libraries these days. I think I spend too much time at your house."

"Seriously? I do not want to think about Grandma Ruby's songs right now. Let's just go."

Nina looked like she was considering it. She glanced at the computer screen. "I still have *eight pages* left on this stupid paper."

That was when the lights went out.

"Worry not, intrepid information seekers! Power should be back on soon." Mr. Dunn lit candles and set out flashlights. "We're on the same power grid as the police station."

They gathered in the main reading area. There were six of them—an old man scowling as he tried to read his newspaper by flashlight, two college students checking the weather on their phones, Mr. Dunn, Nina, and Clark. Nina flopped down in one of the oversized reading chairs.

Clark paced. Shadows played at the light's edges, and they seemed to stew there, churning, like the storm. Like they were coming to life, now that the power was off. Maybe shadows felt more comfortable in dimmer light, because there was more darkness for them to hide in.

When Clark let his eyes unfocus, the shadows at the corners of his eyes took shape, grew tendrils, snapped their jaws.

Eyes glowed behind wolfish shadow-masks.

Without moving his body, Clark cut his eyes to the side, searching the darkness, but as soon as he did, the glowing eyes disappeared. The candlelight quivered, and therefore so did the shadows. They grew and trembled and bled across the ceiling like spilled, living, breathing ink.

"Maybe we ought to get going," said Clark, rubbing his eyes. He vowed to never again stay up until 2 a.m. watching *Noctiluca*. "We can't work on our papers in the dark."

"That's a good idea," Nina said, sounding relieved.

Mr. Dunn was suddenly there, his hand on Clark's shoulder. He had been several yards away, setting up candles, and then he was there, like he'd moved faster than it was possible for people to move.

"Oh," said Mr. Dunn, "you don't want to do that." He smiled, and the candlelight reflected off his glasses. It created the illusion of twin flames dancing where his eyes should have been. "The weather's awful. You'll crash your bikes. You'll fall and hurt yourselves. And then what will your parents think? They'll sue me for letting you leave the library. You're safe here. The storm will pass soon."

Before Clark could protest, Mr. Dunn held out a small plastic container. He opened the lid, revealing stacks of cookies iced white and pink.

"I baked these for our staff party, but I brought too many. We librarians couldn't finish them. We absolutely stuffed ourselves. You can have some, though, if you'd like."

The old man reading his newspaper grumbled to himself. The college students had not looked away from their phones.

"Go on," said Mr. Dunn. "I insist. They're nice and fat and fresh. I like my cookies chewy."

Clark grabbed two, because he wasn't sure what else to do. He wanted to get away from Mr. Dunn, whose eyes he couldn't see. Clark perched on the arm of Nina's chair.

"Here," he said, distracted by the shadows and the glowing eyes at the edge of the room. He gave Nina a cookie, and stuffed the other in his mouth. They had bright jelly filling, and some splattered out onto his jeans.

"Eat it," Clark said, "so he'll leave us alone."

"Fine," said Nina, and popped the other cookie into her mouth. It stained her lips red. "But look." She nodded at the nearest window. Clark looked outside, and he saw the police station, just down the road, and all the houses in between.

Their windows glowed, pouring golden light out into the storm.

"So he lied to us," whispered Nina.

"Obviously. But *why?*" Clark whispered back.

They crouched in an aisle between bookshelves in the 800s section. They had claimed they might as well try to work on their papers. Mr. Dunn had said fine, but don't wander off. Remember, the storm. It's dangerous out there.

"Maybe something's wrong with the library electricity," Nina suggested.

"Yeah, and he doesn't want to scare us. Maybe he called the electric company on his cell phone."

"I bet someone will be out any minute now to get the power back on."

"Definitely. I bet you're right."

Nina sat on the floor, her back against the bookshelves. "I don't feel very good."

"Me neither. We're probably hungry. What time is it, anyway?"

"I don't know. Maybe Mr. Dunn has more of those cookies."

Clark brightened at the thought. "Hey, Nina?"

"Yeah?"

"You see the kids, right? You see the kids in the masks?"

"Yes."

"Up high, on the bookshelves?"

"Yes. They keep running around. They're making those weird clicking noises." Nina put her head in her hands. "They're making me dizzy."

"There are a lot of them now."

"I bet we're just hungry."

"Maybe. You can start to see funny things if you don't eat enough food."

Clark and Nina returned to the reading area, leaving Clark's bag behind. In the small zipper pouch sat a forgotten peanut butter sandwich.

*   *   *

Clark lay with his cheek on the table. His head was full and fuzzy, his mouth dry.

Across from him, Nina licked the icing from her fingers. They had finished Mr. Dunn's cookies. He sat nearby, reading a black book with no title on it, humming a song that Clark recognized. He tried to sing along but couldn't remember the words, and he hadn't yet recovered from the crushing disappointment of realizing there were no cookies left.

Nina kept licking her fingers even once they were clean. She licked her fingers until they were red and chapped and raw. Clark had this nagging feeling that he should ask her if she was all right, that there was something they should do. But every time he tried to speak, the cottony feeling in his mouth took over. He choked on his own swollen, blotchy tongue and nearly threw up, and stopped trying to talk.

The old man and the college students had left. Maybe they had never been there at all. Maybe they were like the kids with the glowing eyes and the masks, watching from the shadows. Maybe this was all a dream, Clark thought.

"Don't worry," said Mr. Dunn from his chair. "We'll get there soon enough. Not much longer now. No, not much longer at all."

Clark wet his cracked lips and looked up. There seemed to be trees now, growing throughout the bookshelves. Tall and dark and crooked, they grew to the ceiling, where the sky was black velvet. There were no stars in this sky, but there was a tiny red moon.

How strange.

The Mandigore, he'll find you
The Mandigore, he smells so sweet
The Mandigore, he wants a treat
The Mandigore, he has a crown

Clark figured he was dreaming, because he was lying on the library floor beneath a canopy of trees, and there was a red moon, and in the branches overhead curled a wide, white snake with ruby eyes.

"My hunters never fail me," said the snake, with the voice of Mr. Dunn. "How swift they are. How clever. They always find such fresh, interesting cuts."

Then the snake slithered away, into a bookshelf, and on the shelf sat rows and rows of black books with no titles. The books grew and elongated and became shadows—child-shadows, with glowing eyes and fierce masks, and they reached for Clark. They drew him into their skinny, cold arms and squeezed and *pulled*. It hurt to be pulled like that, through a surface hard and thorny.

"Clark?" called out Nina, from somewhere far away.

"Clark, where are you?"

"Clark? Is that you?"

The Mandigore, he howls at breakfast
The Mandigore, he howls at night
The Mandigore, he has red meat
The Mandigore, he has white teeth

When Clark awoke, he was pretty sure he wasn't dreaming because his head hurt like crazy.

Pinch me, I must be dreaming. His mouth tasted like vomit, with just a touch of jam filling.

"Ow," he muttered, sitting up. "Nina? What's going on?"

"Don't move, Clark," came Nina's voice. She sounded stressed.

Once Clark opened his eyes, he understood why.

They were in a forest of tall, dark, crooked trees. Above, the sky was velvet black, and there were no stars, but there was a tiny red moon. Throughout the trees, two dozen pairs of glowing eyes stared. Two dozen masks in the shapes of wolves and pigs and goats and birds faced

Clark and Nina, showing off their fangs and their carved pink tongues.

"But I'm awake," Clark said. He pinched himself, and nothing happened. "I don't understand."

"I don't know where we are," said Nina, "but they won't stop singing that *song*. Stop it!" She reached into her pocket and pulled out her *Noctiluca* trading cards, the special edition pack Clark had given her for her birthday.

Nina hesitated, then threw the pack at the masked children. She threw a pen, then a few quarters. Once her pockets were empty, she took off her shoes and threw them, too.

The masked children were swift. Nothing hit them. They moved as the shadows had moved in the library— jumping and darting, dragging themselves from tree root to tree root with long, spindly arms.

And they were singing:

The Mandigore, he'll find you
The Mandigore, he smells so sweet
The Mandigore, he waits for you
The Mandigore, he won't wait long
He won't wait long
He won't wait

Clark took off his shoes, too, and emptied his pockets. He and Nina found pebbles and sticks, and scooped up mud from the forest floor.

The masked children dodged everything thrown at them, and began to laugh as they sang. They took off their masks and beat them against the trees like drums. Their faces were stretched thin, their eyes flat and cold.

The Mandigore, his eyes are keen
The Mandigore, he has a crown
The Mandigore, he says hello
The Mandigore, he says good-bye
Good-bye, good-bye

Nina started to cry, which Clark knew would make her mad, because Nina hated crying. Her *Noctiluca* cards, scattered in the mud, looked pathetic. Captain Farriday's smirking face stared up at them.

"We'd better run," she said. "I don't know where, I don't know what's going on, but—"

"Wait," said Clark, because one of the children had long, pale hair, and freckles across her face, and though her eyes were now black instead of blue, Clark recognized her. He had seen her every day, in the picture frame on Grandma Ruby's nightstand.

"Aunt Mara?"

Aunt Mara tilted her head from side to side, quick and sharp, like a bird.

Clark felt ill; people weren't supposed to move like that. "Aunt Mara, is that you?" He didn't understand it. Aunt Mara had disappeared years and years ago, and yet now here she was, in this forest, beating her goat mask against a tree, looking just as young as she did in that old picture.

"Grandma Ruby went looking for you when you disappeared," Clark said, "but she couldn't find you. Is it seriously you, Aunt Mara? I'm your nephew. My name is Clark. I'm David's son. David, your big brother." He put out his hand, like he might invite a strange cat to say hello. "Do you know where we are? Do you know what happened to us? We were in the library, and the power went out—"

"Clark," Nina whispered, "stop talking to it!"

"Ruby," hissed Aunt Mara. She bit at nothing, her teeth clacking together three times. She spat black liquid onto the ground. "Ruby came. Ruby got away." Aunt Mara smiled. "But you won't."

Aunt Mara threw back her head and let out a horrible rattling sound from the back of her throat. The other children did the same; a chorus of howls filled the forest.

Nina grabbed Clark's hand, and they ran.

They ran until their socks were soaked with blood. It didn't take long; they had lost their shoes, and the ground was sharp with brambles.

They ran with the sounds of clicks and growls and panting at their heels. Aunt Mara's laughter was high and thin like a bird's cry.

They ran even though they had no idea where they were going.

They ran until they found the Mandigore.

The Mandigore wore a dirty golden crown.

He had white teeth in a wide-hinged mouth; when he opened it, his pulpy throat glistened in the light of the red moon.

The Mandigore smelled sweet, like cookies iced pink and white.

The Mandigore had white flames where eyes should have been.

The Mandigore sat sprawled on a pile of bones, his flesh pale, his belly swollen and shiny, his knobby arms and legs draped like never-ending snakes across that pile of bones. His head was too small for his body, too small for that wide, smiling mouth, but the mouth somehow fit anyway.

His jaw cracked and shifted.

He didn't speak, but Clark imagined, if he did, it would sound something like Mr. Dunn. Mr. Dunn, of whom Clark had been *jealous*. This struck him as hysterical, and Clark began to laugh. He laughed so hard he started crying.

And as he laughed, Aunt Mara and the other masked children surrounded them, hissing and clicking their strange language. They hovered in the trees, waiting. What next? What now?

"What are you doing?" Nina screamed. She punched Clark's arm, then his chest. When he didn't respond, she kept punching. "What's wrong with you? Are you insane? Why are you laughing? *Stop laughing.* Calm down! We've got to do something, attack him or—I don't know! We'll just keep running. There's got to be someone here who can help us!"

But there wasn't. Clark knew that, and he knew Nina knew that. It was pretty obvious. It was just like 'Waylaid,' when the *Noctiluca* crew went on that deep-sea exploration mission for Section 47, and they got swarmed by that tribe of giant squid-human mutants, results of a Company experiment gone wrong. Except this time there were no cool TV tricks to get them out in a nice, tidy 45-minute episode.

There was only Clark, and Nina, and a really freaking

terrifying Aunt Mara, who seemed too far gone to be helpful.

Clark thought of Nina's Captain Farriday card, back wherever they had left it, in the mud, filthy and abandoned and smirking to no one in particular.

What would Captain Farriday do?

"When I say go, run," Clark said, straightening. "Run fast, and go throw up somewhere."

Nina stared at him, crying. "*What?*"

"It's those cookies, I bet. The cookies had something in them that brought us here. Run away, throw up, and maybe you'll be able to get away, back to the library."

Nina took off her belt and started whipping it at Aunt Mara, who was creeping closer. *All* the masked children were creeping closer, inching Clark and Nina toward the Mandigore. What had Mr. Dunn said, in Clark's dream? The snake with the voice of Mr. Dunn: *My hunters never fail me.*

Aunt Mara, a hunter for the Mandigore. Clark decided not to think too hard about that; there was no time for more hysterical laughter.

"Just do what I said! I'll keep them distracted." Clark grabbed Nina's hand and squeezed it. "Commander Talia, that's an order."

Nina froze. Her voice was choked. "Captain, are you . . . *crying?*"

"Not important, Commander. Just get out of here." Clark swallowed hard. He didn't want her to see him like this. He wanted her to get home. His parents would give her all his *Noctiluca* gear, he was sure of it. "I'd rather die than have any of my crew get hurt. I'd do anything for them."

"Clark—" Nina whispered.

Clark let go of Nina's hand and started walking toward the Mandigore. He began to sing, shouting the words:

The Mandigore, he'll find you
The Mandigore, he smells so sweet
The Mandigore, he wants a treat
The Mandigore, he has a crown

Aunt Mara stopped growling and lurched back, bouncing back and forth on her knuckles and heels like an ape at the zoo. She shook her head in confusion. The other masked children did the same. They approached Clark, reached out to touch him, and snatched their hands back.

Clark heard Nina tear off into the woods, her bare feet slapping against the ground.

His eyes stung, but he thought of that Captain Farriday

card and tried a smirk of his own. He knew it looked goofy on him; he'd practiced enough in the mirror to know that much. But he figured no one here would care.

> *The Mandigore, he'll find you*
> *The Mandigore, he smells so sweet*
> *The Mandigore, he waits for you*
> *The Mandigore, he won't wait long*
> *He won't wait long*
> *He won't wait*

Aunt Mara and the others were in a frenzy now, howling and hissing, dancing around the Mandigore's pile of bones in a wild circle.

The Mandigore rolled over to face Clark, who had begun climbing up the giant pile of bones. They were sharp, and they gave way under Clark's weight. He was slipping and sliding; the bones cascaded behind him, clattering.

With a lazy groan, the Mandigore smacked his lips and shifted one of his long arms to help Clark up the bone mountain, scooping him toward his open mouth. Clark felt long, rubbery fingers wrap around his left leg.

> *The Mandigore, his eyes are keen*

The Mandigore, he has a crown
The Mandigore, he says hello
The Mandigore, he says good-bye
Good-bye, good-bye

Clark imagined Captain Farriday would probably act like his same cocky self, even at the moment of death, even if he didn't feel cocky at all.

"Why, Mr. Dunn," said Clark, giving the Mandigore a salute, "you've never looked better."

It's true: Guys Read scary stories. And you just proved it. (Unless you just opened the book to this page and started reading. In which case, we feel bad for you because you missed some pretty scary stuff.)

Now what?

Now we keep going—Guys Read keeps working to find good stuff for you to read, and you read it and pass it along to other guys. Here's how we can do it:

For more than ten years, Guys Read has been at www.guysread.com, collecting recommendations of what guys really want to read. We have gathered recommendations of thousands of great funny books, scary books, action books, illustrated books, information books, wordless books, sci-fi books, mystery books, and you-name-it books.

So what's your part of the job? Simple: Try out some of the suggestions at guysread.com, try some of the other stuff written by the authors in this book, and then let us know what you think. Tell us what you like to read. Tell us what you don't like to read. The more you tell us, the more great book recommendations we can collect. It might even help us choose the writers for the next installment of Guys Read.

Thanks for reading.

And thanks for helping Guys Read.

JON SCIESZKA (editor) has been writing books for children ever since he took time off from his career as an elementary school teacher. He wanted to create funny books that kids would want to read. Once he got going, he never stopped. He is the author of numerous picture books, middle grade series, and even a memoir. From 2007–2010 he served as the first National Ambassador for Young People's Literature, appointed by the Library of Congress. Since 2004, Jon has been actively promoting his interest in getting boys to read through his Guys Read initiative and website. Born in Flint, Michigan, Jon now lives in Brooklyn with his family. Visit him online at www.jsworldwide.com and at www.guysread.com.

SELECTED TITLES

THE TRUE STORY OF THE THREE LITTLE PIGS
(Illustrated by Lane Smith)

THE STINKY CHEESE MAN AND OTHER FAIRLY STUPID TALES
(Illustrated by Lane Smith)

The Time Warp Trio series, including SUMMER READING
IS KILLING ME! (Illustrated by Lane Smith)

The Frank Einstein series, including FRANK EINSTEIN AND
THE ANTIMATTER MOTOR (Illustrated by Brian Biggs)

BATTLE BUNNY
(with Mac Barnett, illustrated by Matt Myers)

KELLY BARNHILL ("Don't Eat the Baby") is a former teacher, former bartender, former waitress, former activist, former park ranger, former wildland firefighter, former secretary, former janitor, and former church-guitar-player. Everything she has done up to now has prepared her for her current job of telling stories. She has published three novels (with several more in the works) and also teaches in a community arts program in her home state of Minnesota. Visit her online at www.kellybarnhill.wordpress.com/work.

SELECTED TITLES

THE WITCH'S BOY

THE MOSTLY TRUE STORY OF JACK

IRON HEARTED VIOLET

MICHAEL BUCKLEY ("Mr. Shocky") managed to survive a tragic accident in which he was bombarded with gamma radiation. Days later, he awoke to discover he had changed. Now, when he gets mad, he changes into an enormous green monster people call "The Hulk." He faked his own death and will stay that way until he learns to control the savage monster within him. Oh, wait. That's the biography for Bruce Banner. Never mind. Michael Buckley grew up in Akron, Ohio. In case you are taking notes, this is nowhere near any lab where gamma radiation research was going on. He is a former roller boogie fanatic, but maintains that this does not make him a monster . . . even if there were a few injuries when he would "shoot the duck."

ADAM GIDWITZ ("The Blue-Bearded Bird-Man") was born in San Francisco but moved to Baltimore, where he grew up going to a school without many rules. Even so, he managed to break all of them, spending his entire middle school career in the principal's office. Surprisingly, he went on to become a teacher. He also started to meet writers and to read bags full of children's books. He lives in Brooklyn. Visit him online at www.adamgidwitz.com.

ADELE GRIFFIN and **LISA BROWN** ("Manifest") have worked together for years. Adele is a two-time National Book Award finalist and highly acclaimed author of a number of books for young adult and middle grade readers. Lisa draws illustrations and comics, writes books and book reviews, and teaches kids and college students. She has also published a ton of books. Together Adele and Lisa created PICTURE THE DEAD, a traditional ghost story with a visual twist. The visual clues allow the reader to unravel the mystery in step (or ahead of) the narrator. The pictures are based on old photographs from the nineteenth century. Find out more about Adele at www.adelegriffin.com. Find out more about Lisa at www.americanchickens.com.

GRIS GRIMLY (illustrator) has been drawing since he was old enough to hold a pencil. He is inspired by music, films, fantastical images, plays, concerts, monsters, and writers such as Edgar Allan Poe, Edward Gorey, and H. P. Lovecraft. Gris moonlights as a filmmaker, fine artist, and concept designer, but his heart will always be in children's illustration. Visit him online at www.madcreator.com.

SELECTED TITLES

GRIS GRIMLY'S FRANKENSTEIN

EDGAR ALLEN POE'S TALES OF MYSTERY AND MADNESS

GRIS GRIMLY'S WICKED NURSERY RHYMES

THE DANGEROUS ALPHABET (Written by Neil Gaiman)

CLAIRE LEGRAND's ("The Mandigore") first novel is THE CAVENDISH HOME FOR BOYS AND GIRLS, a New York Public Library Best Book for Children in 2012. She is also the author of THE YEAR OF SHADOWS and WINTERSPELL, a young adult retelling of *The Nutcracker*. She is one of the four authors behind THE CABINET OF CURIOSITIES anthology, a Junior Library Guild selection and a New York Public Library Best Book for Children in 2014. Visit her at www.claire-legrand.com and at www.enterthecabinet.com.

NIKKI LOFTIN ("Licorice Needles") lives with her family just outside Austin, Texas, surrounded by dogs, goats, and small, loud boys. She has been a popcorn seller, waitress, bookstore employee, music and gifted/talented teacher, and a director of family ministries. Her favorite food/obsession is ice cream, preferably Blue Bell Moo-llennium Crunch. On very good days, she prefers writing even to ice cream. Visit her online at www.nikkiloftin.com.

SELECTED TITLES

WISH GIRL

THE SINISTER SWEETNESS OF SPLENDID ACADEMY

NIGHTINGALE'S NEST

DANIEL JOSÉ OLDER ("Marcos at the River") is a writer, editor, and musician. His band, Ghost Star, gigs regularly around New York, and he runs storytelling workshops. He has also worked as a paramedic in New York City. Find him online at www.ghoststar.net.

SELECTED TITLES

HALF-RESURRECTION BLUES

SHADOWSHAPER

SALSA NOCTURNA

DAV PILKEY ("My Ghost Story") has spent his life trying to make kids laugh . . . and getting into trouble. At the age of four, Dav was kicked out of "Safety School" for throwing stuff out the window. Thus began a spree of mischievousness that has lasted his entire life. In elementary school, Dav was a responsible kid—whenever anything bad happened, Dav was responsible. And whenever Dav did anything bad, his teacher would snap her fingers, send him to the hallway, pointing to the door, and shout: "Mr. Pilkey—OUT!" Dav always kept his hallway desk well stocked. It was in the hallway that Dav had his first experiences making up stories and illustrating them, and he has never stopped. He lives in Washington State. Visit him online at www.pilkey.com.

R.L. STINE ("Disappear!") has a great job: "To give kids the CREEPS!" His books are read all over the world. So far, he has sold over 350 million books, making him one of the bestselling children's authors in history. He always liked scary movies and books. When he was about eight or nine, he started reading scary horror comic books. He and his brother went to every scary movie. They never got scared. They always laughed. He has written over 300 books. He has never seen a ghost. But he keeps looking. Visit him online at www.rlstine.com.

SELECTED TITLES

The Fear Street series, including PARTY GAMES

The Goosebumps Most Wanted series, including THE 12 SCREAMS OF CHRISTMAS

The Goosebumps Hall of Horror series, including THE BIRTHDAY PARTY OF NO RETURN!

NIGHTMARE HOUR: *Time for Terror*

RITA WILLIAMS-GARCIA ("Coconut Heads") is the author of several award-winning novels. Known for their realistic portrayals of teens of color, Williams-Garcia's works have been recognized by the Coretta Scott King Award committee, PEN/Norma Klein, American Library Association, and Parents' Choice, among others. She was born in Queens, New York. She learned to read early and was aware of events as she grew up in the 60s. In the midst of real events, she daydreamed and wrote stories. Writing stories for young people is her passion and her mission. Visit her online at www.rwg.com.

Jon Scieszka presents
THE GUYS READ LIBRARY
OF GREAT READING

Volume 1

Volume 2

Volume 3

Volume 4

Volume 5

Volume 6

How many have *you* read?

WALDEN POND PRESS™
An Imprint of HarperCollins*Publishers*

www.harpercollinschildrens.com
www.walden.com/books